What Skylar Needs

Copyright © 2018 Lanee Lane

All rights reserved. No part of this publication may be reproduced, distributed, or transmitted in any form or by any means, including photocopying, recording, or other electronic or mechanical methods, without the prior written permission of the publisher, except in the case of brief quotations embodied in critical reviews and certain other noncommercial uses permitted by copyright law. For permission requests, write to the publisher, addressed "Attention: Permissions Coordinator," at the address below.

Cover Art by goonwrite.com

Table of Content

Chapter One

Chapter Two

Chapter Three

Chapter Four

Chapter Five

Chapter Six

Chapter Seven

Chapter Eight

Chapter Nine

Chapter Ten

Chapter Eleven

Chapter Twelve

Chapter Thirteen

Chapter Fourteen

Chapter Fifteen

Chapter Sixteen

Chapter Seventeen

Chapter Eighteen

Chapter Nineteen

Chapter Twenty

Chapter Twenty-One

Chapter Twenty-Two

Chapter Twenty-Three

Chapter Twenty-Four

Chapter Twenty-Five

Chapter Twenty-Six

Epilogue

Dedication

To my mom: Thank you for sharing your love of books with me and always believing in me.

CHAPTER ONE

Skylar turned up the sound on the T.V. He was trying to have a relaxing Sunday evening of football and beer with his brother. His neighbor apparently had other plans.

"A new chick moved in upstairs. That must be her listening to her teenybopper music. Don't people have any respect for their neighbors anymore?"

"I don't know, bro; guess not. You could take a broomstick to the ceiling. You know, like the movies," Brendon answered back.

Skylar got up from the couch and grabbed the broom from the kitchen. Back in the living room, he banged the broomstick on the ceiling a few times. The music turned down, so he set the broom beside the T.V. and reclaimed his seat on the couch. The Bears were playing, and he didn't want any distractions while watching his team. He was taking a pull of his beer when the music started back up even louder this time. Then there were loud thuds.

"What the hell is she doing up there? Is she running freaking laps in her living room?" Skylar growled out.

"Sounds like more than one person, bro. Maybe she's having a party."

"I don't care if she is having a party! I'm trying to watch the game. I'm going up there to tell her what she can do with her party and her music."

"Tell me if she's hot or has hot friends up there. I'd be willing to join them."

Skylar rolled his eyes at his brother. Hot or not, she was going to get an earful. He slipped on his slides and headed out the door toward the stairs. He took the stairs two at a time, his annoyance mounting with every step. *What a waste of my time*, he thought. *Normal people had common courtesy, but nooo, not my new neighbor. She just had to be a boy-band-loving disturbance.*

At her door, he knocked with three loud raps. He could hear voices and the music turned down a bit. The door swung open and a short woman with brown skin and curly black hair stood before him. She smiled up at him and for a moment he forgot he was even angry.

"Hi, you must be the pizza guy. If you want to step in for a second, I'll go grab my wallet."

Leaving the door open she turned to get her wallet. Was this chick serious? For one, he didn't have any pizzas in his hands. Two, who just left their door open for complete strangers even if they were the pizza guy? He stepped into the threshold waiting for her to return. The pizza guy walked up at the same time she reappeared. When she looked up from her wallet, there was a look of confusion on her face.

"Good evening," the man with the pizzas said. "I have one pepperoni, one supreme and an order of cheese bread. Your total is thirty-two even."

She handed the guy two twenties.

"You guys training tonight?" the curly haired half pint asked.

"Um, no," the pizza man said. "I'm out delivering by myself tonight."

She looked over at Skylar. "Huh, so who are you then?"

"I'm your neighbor."

"Well howdy, neighbor!" she said as a big smile spread across her face. "Come on in. You can join us for pizza if you want. I moved in this week and I haven't met anyone from the building yet."

She took the pizzas from the pizza guy's arms and thanked him. She turned into her apartment and once again left her door open for him to follow. This time he followed. He'd come up here on a mission, and he was going to say what he came to say. It didn't matter that she was clearly oblivious to his annoyed mood and that her smile was friendly and inviting. He wasn't here to make friends. The mission was to get some quiet for his football viewing.

In the kitchen, he saw two other women gabbing at his new neighbor. One had fiery red hair and was a few inches taller. The other was the tallest of them all with straight brown hair and freckles scattered across her cheeks and nose.

After a moment, they turned and noticed him. The one with the red hair looked him up and down. There was no shame in her ogling. He went out to local clubs all the time and had a pretty active social life. Women checked him out all the time. He wasn't conceited, but he thought he was a good-looking guy. Anything he may lack in looks, which he doubted was much, he made up for in his physique. He prided himself on keeping in shape. Running was part of his morning routine and he liked to hit the weights a few times a week as well.

"Helloooo, handsome. To what do we owe this pleasure?" Red asked.

"Good grief, Claudia, must you be such a floozy?" His neighbor asked while swatting the redhead on her behind.

What the hell had he walked into?

"Ladies, this is my new neighbor. I invited him to have pizza with us."

"Ugh, Melanie! You know this is supposed to be a man-free zone tonight," Red whined.

"Claud, I know, but I can't exactly be rude to my new neighbor. I need to make a good impression."

The ladies carried on for a moment as if he wasn't even in the room. He snorted at what Melanie, as he now knew her as, had said. *Too late*, he thought, *you already blew the first impression out of the water and not in a good way, lady*. As for rude, she had kind of killed that one as well with the loud pop music seeping through his ceiling.

"Do you have a name, neighbor?" Claudia asked.

Skylar was not sure how he had gotten pulled into a full out conversation with these women. He'd simply gone up there to tell them to keep it down. He could have said what he needed to from the door. He needed to tell them the deal and get out of here. Alas, he could tell it wasn't going to be that easy.

"Skylar. My name's Skylar."

Indifference was obvious in his tone. He didn't want them to get the idea that he was being friendly or wanted to make small talk.

"That's a nice name, Skylar. I'm Claudia, and this is Jade," she pointed to the woman with freckles. "This here is my BFF and your neighbor, Melanie. She is single and ready to mingle by the way." She waggled her eyebrows at him suggestively.

"Claudia!" Melanie slapped a hand over her friend's mouth, and Claudia let out a big belly laugh.

"I'm so sorry, Skylar. She recently had surgery to remove her foot from her mouth, but there is some recovery time."

As she let go of her friend's mouth, there was another knock at the door. The ladies looked at each other wondering who could be at the door. Melanie left the kitchen to go see who it was. The door opened and Skylar heard a familiar voice.

"Hi, is Skylar here?"

A moment later, Brendon walked into the kitchen. Skylar shook his head. This was getting out of control. He was missing the game because of these three.

"What are you doing here, Brendon? I told you I would be right back."

"Dude, you were taking forever. I came to make sure you were still alive and didn't get lost."

"I'm fine," he said through gritted teeth.

"Who are you?" Claudia asked Brendon.

"Oh, sorry for my manners, ladies. I'm Brendon, Skylar's brother."

"Makes sense, you're pretty easy on the eyes like your brother."

To Skylar's dismay, his brother flashed what he called his 'panty-wetting' smile. For fuck's sake, why couldn't his brother have stayed downstairs? At this rate, they would never get to watch the game.

"Brendon, I just invited Skylar to stay for pizza. You are welcome to join us if you'd like," Melanie said as she handed him a paper plate.

"Well, if it's not too much trouble, I'd love to."

Skylar rolled his eyes. His brother was such a traitor. A few women and some pizza and he abandoned their football game for a girls' night. If Melanie pulled out a beer, he thought his brother might ask to move in. Now he was stuck. If he left and his brother stayed, he would look like a jerk. If he stayed, he was going to be in a shit mood.

"Come on, man, we have a game to watch. I bought snacks for us to eat."

"Uh yeah, but you don't have pizza and pretty ladies," Brendon said as he bit into a slice of supreme pizza.

"Whatever, man, I'm going to go watch the game."

"Come on, big guy. Why don't you stay and hang with us? We are about to start the karaoke back up. You can have the first song." This came from Claudia, who was sitting awfully close to Brendon.

"No, I came up here to ask you to turn the music down. I'm trying to watch the game and you guys are up here listening to teenybopper songs and stomping around."

"Excuse me, but we weren't stomping. We were doing choreographed moves," Melanie said with a look of shock.

She had the nerve to truly look taken aback at the fact he would call their dancing 'stomping'. This chick was really touched.

"I am sorry that we were disrupting your game. We were just breaking in my new apartment and having a breakup party. We'll try to keep it down from now on."

Skylar gave a curt nod.

"I'd appreciate it."

With that, he walked out of her apartment leaving his turncoat brother behin

CHAPTER TWO

Melanie sat up and turned her alarm clock off for the fifth time. After her 'girls' night-turned-coed' party, she was tired. Thankfully, she didn't have to be at work too early. Picking her schedule was a perk to having the most seniority at the boutique.

She shopped for, and styled, women of all shapes and sizes, but her passion was helping other plus size women like herself. Being a size sixteen, she knew what it was like to struggle to find fashionable clothes that she loved.

In the kitchen, she put the kettle on to brew her green tea. The aftermath of her get-together was everywhere. Empty pizza boxes and glasses littered her kitchen island. She took a few minutes to put the boxes in the trash and add the cups to her dishwasher. While her teakettle warmed, she ran her trash down to the dumpster.

As she was walking out the door to the apartment building, she came face to face with none other than her neighbor. He was shirtless. His skin was damp from what she assumed was sweat. His body was solid, and she had the sudden urge to wrap her hand around his bicep and squeeze. Realizing she was staring, she spoke up.

"Hi, nice to see you again." She offered up her best smile, but the face looking back at her didn't return it. "The weather is nice today. Seems like it's finally starting to heat up again."

More staring from him. *Tough crowd*, she thought. Glancing up at him, she realized just how tall he was. He towered over her five-foot two-inch frame. The grim look glaring back at her was a bit intimidating. A nervous laugh escaped her.

"I guess I'll just scoot on by you. Have a good day." Flashing another smile that she was sure looked like a grimace, she slipped past him. When she was about halfway to the dumpster she looked over her shoulder to see if he was still there. Sure enough, he was. She wiggled her fingers in a wave and hightailed it the rest of the way.

Two hours later, she walked into work ready to take her first client. The client was a woman she had worked with a few times before. There were files for each of her clients with their style preferences on her computer at the boutique. It was important to Melanie that the women she worked with were comfortable and confident with her abilities.

There was a light knock on her door, and she looked up to find her boss, Barbara, standing there. Black, tailored slacks covered her bottom half and were paired with a bright, abstract kimono top. Her brown bob was straightened to perfection. She was so elegant.

"Hey, Barbara. How are you today?"

"I'm doing well, darling. I've just been scouting out some new designers we may want to carry in the boutique."

That was one of the things Melanie loved most about Barbara and Finesse & Flare. She tried to give up-and-coming designers a chance to get their work out there. There were several designers that had been featured in their little boutique that were now doing very well for themselves. Melanie would often feature them on her blog as a way to have unique styles as well.

"Find anyone that's tickled your fancy yet?"

"There are a few with some potential, but we'll see."

The two spoke for a few more minutes before Melanie went back to preparing for her client. She flipped through the pages, making a mental list of what they had in stock that would suit her. It didn't take long to set up her plan of attack. She grabbed a clothing rack from the back room and began to place items on to it. Once she had enough pieces, she wheeled it to the front just as her client was coming in.

With a warm smile, she greeted her client. They were an upscale boutique, so they had an assistant that offered drinks and snacks during their appointments. The woman was shopping for a vacation with her boyfriend, and she wanted to look 'smoking hot' in her own words. She confided that she thought he may pop the question on the trip so she needed everything from a classy evening dress to slinky lingerie.

Melanie was able to help her find the perfect wardrobe for her potential pending engagement. Getting to help women feel and look good for so many important moments in life was her favorite part of the job. The client promised to bring back pictures from her trip as she left the boutique.

The rest of Melanie's day quickly passed. She had five more clients that day, and in between appointments she helped the walk-in customers and posted on her social media sites. Sites like Instagram were good for both blog traffic and actual business. She'd been considering doing some independent personal styling, but hadn't quite made the jump. When she decided to do that, she would have no problem finding clients. Her inbox was filled with multiple emails a week inquiring if she did any personal styling.

When seven o'clock rolled around, she and Barbara locked up the shop and headed to their cars. Since it was a slow evening, they were able to get all of the closing tasks done before seven.

"Any big plans tonight, love?"

"No. You know me; just working on some blog posts and then curling up with a book."

"Darling, you are too young to be living your life through romance novels. You have to get out and live for yourself. Find yourself a real-life romance."

This was a lecture that Melanie had heard many times from her boss. The older woman had been married to her husband for thirty years. Of course, she thought it was as easy as just going out and finding someone; she hadn't dated in forever. Melanie had a news flash for her; dating in this day in age was hard. Adding a plus size figure to the equation made it even harder. She'd rather live in a fantasy world than dive into the fiery pits of Tinder.

"Not everyone is as lucky as you to have found the love of their life at twenty-two, Barbara. Maybe the old maid life is for me."

"No, Mel, it's not. You are much too beautiful of a girl, inside and out, to be alone. Your Prince Charming is going to come and, when he does, I can't wait to witness it."

On her way home, Melanie thought about what Barb had said. Her mind wandered to her brooding neighbor. He was living proof that she did not have the desired effect on men. He nearly burned a hole in her giving her the stare-down that morning. Maybe she deserved it. They had kind of interrupted his quiet with their karaoke night. They didn't mean any harm; just a little girl fun. Plus, she invited him to stay. How much nicer could she have been?

She decided to stop at a local deli to grab something for dinner. Most nights, she enjoyed cooking. Monday's were her exception. Inside the deli, she ordered a warm panini and soup. A case full of baked goods lined the wall and she made a spur of the moment decision.

Twenty minutes later, she was knocking on Skylar's door. She didn't know what the hell possessed her to do so, but there she stood with a vanilla cupcake in hand. Voices and movement came from behind the door. After what felt like several minutes, the door finally opened. The face that greeted her was not Skylar's.

A tall blonde stood in the door of Skylar's apartment. She had piercing green eyes, toned legs that were showcased in a short black skirt, and perky breasts that were quite exposed by her V-neck top. She was stunning and was Melanie's polar opposite.

"Um, hi. I'm Melanie, the neighbor. I came to speak to Skylar."

The blonde stood there staring at Melanie. Sizing her up as if she was trying to figure out what the hell a short, black woman was doing at his door. Why hadn't Melanie thought about the fact that he may have a girlfriend and a live-in one at that? Of course he did. He may be mean, but he was sexy. That couldn't be denied.

Before the blonde responded, Melanie heard Skylar ask her who it was before appearing in the doorway. When he saw it was her, his expression went blank.

"Candace, go ahead and relax on the couch. I poured you some wine. I'll be right there."

Candace gave Melanie one last look before turning to Skylar. She wrapped her arms around his neck and kissed him.

"Don't be long," she said releasing his neck and retreating into the apartment. Skylar turned his gaze back to Melanie.

"What do you want?"

Despite his attitude, she smiled. She wanted to take the cupcake and shove it in his sexy face but refrained, knowing that it would not solve anything. Instead, she decided to woman up and apologize. Even if she didn't think he deserved one.

"I thought we got off on the wrong foot. I wanted to bring a peace offering as an 'I'm Sorry' gift. We are going to be neighbors, and I don't want you hating me the entire time. I brought you a cupcake as my white flag."

He looked at the cupcake and back up at her. He wondered why she cared if he liked her or not. This was life, and not everyone was going to like you. When he looked at her she seemed so hopeful and sincere. Being mean to her now felt like being mean to a puppy.

"Fine, I accept your peace offering. Just keep it down from now on; at least on game nights."

"No problem. I'll be as quiet as a mouse."

She smiled up at him and lifted her hands to offer the cupcake. Her smile was beautiful. It wasn't manufactured by thousands of dollars of dental work. A small gap in her two front teeth gave it character. He accepted the cupcake and waited for her to end whatever it was they were doing.

"Ok then," she said, "I guess I'll let you get back to your date. I'll see you around, neighbor."

"Yeah, see you around."

She spun on her heels and made her way up the stairs.

CHAPTER THREE

"Oohhhh, Skylar!" Bang, bang, bang. "I'm so close."

This had been going on for thirty minutes and Melanie had had enough. To think she had been worried about being loud and disturbing Skylar. She brought him a peace offering for goodness' sake and this.... THIS was how he repaid her? Loud monkey sex with, she assumed, the buxom blonde from earlier. Didn't he know people had jobs and wanted to sleep?

Their grunts, moans and overall screeches were distracting. Not to mention that it sounded like the man could go all night. Couldn't he get off already so she could have some peace? She picked up her phone from the bedside table and sent a group text to Claudia and Jade.

Melanie: My neighbor, Mr. Grumpypants, seems to be having a party of his own tonight.

Claudia: You should go crash it.

Jade: Claud, that would be rude.

Melanie: It's not that kinda party. He and some blonde bombshell type are going at it like rabbits. I've heard her scream more times than I can count. #barf

Claudia: Then you should definitely crash that party. Mr. Grumpy pants is sexy. Ask to join the fun.

Jade: How do you know she is a "blonde bombshell"?

Claudia: Good point J. How do you know this?

Melanie: Long story, but I saw her at his apartment earlier today.

Claudia: Well if he has her screaming like that then maybe you should get in his good graces. You could use a little ride on his motorcycle.

Jade: Really?!

Melanie: Goodnight creeper.

* * *

Skylar plopped down on the couch. He'd just walked Candace out. He could tell that she wanted to stay overnight, but he didn't want to give her the wrong impression. They both agreed from the start that this would only be about sex; no commitment, and no sleepovers. He was afraid that she had forgotten the rules and was getting attached.

Skylar enjoyed the sex they had, but he wasn't looking for anything serious. His career was his main focus. Love and relationships just didn't fit into that right now. He had a feeling it was time to cut things off with Candace. It would suck because what they had worked for him, but he didn't need her catching feelings. If she did that, then he'd never get rid of her.

After flipping through the channels, he turned the T.V. off and headed to bed. He had to be up early. He was visiting a new business tomorrow that he would begin consulting work with. The company he worked for, Brenshasw Consulting, helped many businesses and focused on start-ups and newer businesses.

While he lay in bed, his neighbor popped into his head. She brought him a cupcake. Who did that kind of thing? Who went out of their way to give someone a peace offering? Especially someone who had been as cold as he had been to her? He kind of felt bad for acting like such a jerk. She looked so innocent standing there with a cupcake in hand and what seemed like sincere intentions.

Melanie was a stark contrast to Candace. She was petite. He doubted she was much more than five feet tall. Her skin was a warm brown color, her hair a mass of tightly coiled curls, and she had curves for days. Despite having had his fair share of model type women, he definitely could acknowledge that she was beautiful. What man didn't appreciate full hips, breasts and a round behind?

Skylar tried to shake her out of his head. He had no idea why he would be thinking of her in the bed that he had just had sex with Candace in. Melanie was his neighbor, and he was never going there with her. As a matter of fact, he didn't plan on even seeing her except in passing. Closing his eyes, he waited for sleep to take over.

The next morning, Skylar headed out of his apartment to his car and was running through his talking points on a presentation he would be giving later that day. As he neared the car, he saw Melanie standing by hers. She had the hood open and was just staring at the engine block. The urge to avert his eyes and act like he never saw her was strong. He didn't have time to deal with whatever her issue was, but his manners got the best of him and he walked toward her.

"Car trouble?"

"You could say that," she replied without looking up at him.

"What's going on with it?"

"I don't know. If I did, I wouldn't be standing here staring at it."

So, the sweet neighbor has a bit of a snarky side, he noted.

"Obviously," he rolled his eyes even though he knew she wasn't paying attention. "What happens when you try to turn it on?"

"Nothing. It makes a revving sound and then nothing."

"I can try to jump it to see if that works. Maybe it's just the battery." She finally gave him a sideways glance.

"Ok. Thanks."

"Do you have jumper cables?"

"Um, no. I don't think so."

Skylar huffed out a breath. "You should always have jumper cables. It should be a part of your car essentials kit."

"Car essentials kit? I put gas in it when it gets low. What more do I need to do?"

Instead of answering her question, Skylar walked toward his car. He pulled it up beside hers and pulled the cables from the trunk.

"Come over here and pay attention," Skylar said over his shoulder.

He heard her mutter something about 'bossy' under her breath, but he ignored it. Everyone needed to know the basics of a car if they were going to drive one, and jumping a car was an essential. Mustering all of his patience, he talked her through how to do it. To his surprise, she seemed really receptive to learning. Their attempt to jump the car was in vain. The car was still reluctant to turn over.

"Hmm, must not be your battery then. You're probably going to have to get it towed to a shop."

"Great. Just great." She kicked her foot against the car.

"Whoa, there. Wouldn't want you to do more damage than you've already done."

"I don't have time for my car to be breaking down. I have a job that I have to get to every day."

"Do you have Triple A?"

"No."

"Where do you work?"

"Downtown, at a boutique."

Skylar looked up at the sky and heaved out a breath. "Ok, I can drop you off at work. It's on my way. You can figure out what to do about your car tonight or something."

"I can't ask you to do that. I can take an Uber."

Skylar pressed the bridge of his nose with his fingers. *Why couldn't she just agree and make things simple?*

"Melanie, it's fine. It's no trouble. Please, just get in the car."

She crossed her arms over her chest and stalked to the car. He walked around to her side and opened the door for her. The frown on her face deepened. Geez, he tried to be nice to the woman and she radiated disdain. This was exactly why he didn't want a relationship.

He walked around to his side of the car and braced himself for the ice storm. Inside the car, he turned on some music and started to back out of the lot.

"Thank you."

He turned and looked at her briefly. She had loosened her arms from around her chest. If he was honest, he was kind of glad she'd stopped that. She did have a really nice rack, and her crossed arms only brought more attention to it. Not that he would ever act on any of his thoughts.

"You're welcome."

They drove in silence. Melanie looked out of the window at the passing buildings. She couldn't help but think that this day was shaping up to be terrible already. She was thinking about when she would have time to call repair shops. She only had a few appointments today, so that should leave her time to call around.

When they pulled up to her job, she was ready to bolt from the car. She was thankful for the ride, but she still wasn't Skylar's biggest fan. Another 'thank you' was on her tongue, but he spoke before she got a chance.

"What time do you get off?"

"Six. Why?"

"I'll be here."

Melanie was surprised. She didn't expect him to pick her up. Heck, she hadn't expected a ride to work.

"Oh, no. That isn't necessary. I'll have Jade or Claudia pick me up or catch an Uber. You've done enough."

"We're going to the same place. I'll be here at six."

Melanie stared at him. His jaw was set, and it looked like he was clenching his teeth. His hands had a death grip on the steering wheel. She wasn't sure why he insisted if he was going to look so angry about it.

"Fine. Thank you again."

She hurried out of the car. He sure seemed grumpy all of the time. Or maybe he was just grumpy around her. Who knew? Honestly, at that moment, she didn't have much time to care.

Once she was in her office, she turned on her computer to check her appointments for the day. There would be working the floor, and doing follow-up calls with clients.

Since it was a little before nine, she decided to search Google to find a few auto repair places to call. Several calls later, she settled on a shop that had good reviews and could tow her car for a reasonable price. The tow truck would be at her house at seven the next morning. By the time she got home that night, the shop wouldn't be open anyway.

Jade walked into her office as she was hanging up with the auto shop.

"Morning," Jade said plopping down on the chair across the desk with her signature caramel latte in hand.

"Hey, girl. What's up?"

"Nothing really. Trying to suck down this coffee so I'm not a zombie all day."

"I could bypass the coffee and go straight for shots after the morning I've had."

"Oh, no. What happened?"

Melanie gave her a recap of her morning.

"That really sucks, Mel. I hope, whatever it is, it's an easy fix. I could take you home. If you want me to pick you up for work in the morning, I can do that too."

"I hate to have you come all the way to get me, but that would be really great. I have no idea how long it will take to fix my car."

"No problem, I don't mind at all."

The day went by quickly. When the time rolled around to a quarter to six she heard Jade greet a customer. It was getting close to being time to leave, and since she was catching a ride she couldn't really help any last-minute customers.

"Is Melanie still here?" she heard a deep voice ask.

She made her way to the counter where he was standing with Jade.

"I'm here, but I still have fifteen minutes," she said as she approached.

"I'm aware of what time it is. I wanted to make sure you didn't run off early so you didn't have to ride with me."

"Although that is a good idea, kudos to you for thinking of it, I did not run off." She rolled her eyes. He really pushed her buttons.

"I can see that."

"Jade here could have taken me home. She is going to pick me up in the morning, so you will be relieved of your duties."

He arched a brow at her and gave her a look like she was crazy. "Why?"

It was her turn to give him a look.

"Why what?"

"Why would she give you a ride in the morning when we live in the same building?"

"Because she is my friend and you and I are not friends. I don't want to keep asking you for favors."

"You aren't asking for favors," he replied, and she resisted the urge to stomp her foot.

"Whatever, you know what I mean. I don't want to burden you or owe you."

He stared down at her. She returned the stare, refusing to back down from his intense gaze.

"Has anyone ever told you that you are exhausting?"

A smile crept up on her face. "All the more reason not to drive me."

He ran a hand down his handsome face and then looked to Jade.

"Don't worry about picking her up in the morning. No need for you to go out of your way. I'll bring Crazy to work tomorrow."

"Hey, I resent that," Mel protested.

He ignored her and waited for Jade's acknowledgment. She looked back and forth between Melanie and Skylar. Skylar kept a stone cold face while Melanie kept motioning with her thumb across her neck.

"Ok," Jade finally said.

Skylar looked at Melanie. "See, it isn't that hard to be agreeable."

Turning his back from the front counter, he headed toward one of the chairs in front of the window. He began scrolling through his phone like he didn't just come into her place of business and make demands. The man was infuriating.

CHAPTER FOUR

Melanie took her time reorganizing clothes, cleaning the windows, and doing other closing duties. Maybe he'd get impatient and decide he didn't want to take her tomorrow. When she'd done everything she could think of, she went to the back and grabbed her purse. For added effect, she stood in her office an extra few minutes opening and closing desk draws just to take up more time.

When she emerged, he was in the same spot. Now his arms were crossed, and his stare was pinned on her. She gave him an innocent smile.

"All set," she said not letting the smile drop from her face.

"Are you sure? Any more windows to clean?" The sarcasm in his voice was heavy.

Batting her eyes, she replied, "Nope, all done. Let's go." She turned to Jade and gave her a wave and walked out.

Skylar gave Jade an exasperated look before he followed behind Melanie. Jade offered a small smile and shrugged her shoulders. He knew then that Melanie was a lot of sass in a tiny package.

He eased into traffic. A light rock station was playing on low. Melanie began flipping through channels until it landed on a pop station.

"What are you doing?" His hands tightened on the steering wheel. Hadn't this woman ever heard that you don't mess with a man's radio?

"What do you mean what am I doing?" Her head was bobbing to the beat of a popular boy band.

"Why did you just change my station?"

"Because I needed some jams." She snapped her fingers and sang along. Her voice was off key, but she was giving it her all.

Skylar glanced over at her. There was no shame in her jam session. He'd bet she was the type of person who thrived at karaoke bars. Giving up on the radio battle, he focused on the road while trying to tune out the awful sound.

"You hungry?"

She didn't say anything at first, but when he looked over at her, he saw she had her head cocked looking at him.

"What?" he asked.

"I'm trying to figure you out."

"What do you mean?"

"One minute you can't stand me and you roll your eyes at me constantly. The next minute you're offering me rides and opening doors. I should say demanding to give me rides, but you get the picture. I don't get you."

"There's nothing to get. Your car broke. I have a car. I need to eat. You need to eat. It's rather simple actually. I was raised to have manners. You, I'm not so sure."

"Heeey! I have plenty of manners. It's kind of hard to know when to use them when you're dealing with a moody, bossy man."

He scoffed at that. "You are delusional, sweetheart. I'm not moody or bossy. I'm chivalrous. You just seem to know how to push my buttons.."

"Whatever you say, bossy-pants."

Skylar pulled into a Chinese restaurant that was about five minutes from their building. As he was getting out of the car, he said, "Either come in or get whatever I choose." Then he closed the door.

She wanted to strangle him, but she figured that explaining that he was a bossy jerk wouldn't fly as an excuse with the police. Instead, she got out and ran to catch up with him. Inside, he ordered several things off of the menu and then asked her what she wanted. She knew what she wanted, but she took her time looking. She knew that it would drive him crazy, and that had become her new favorite game.

"Ok," he finally gritted out. "Pick something now or you get nothing."

"No need to be so impatient unless, of course, you have another long night ahead of you with the blonde bombshell."

Skylar's neck and cheeks started to turn pink.

"My nights are none of your concern."

"They are when I can hear every 'Oh Skylar, right there' from the comfort of my own bed."

He didn't reply to her last comment. It wasn't like the ceiling was very thick in their building. He had heard some of his own neighbors during their tussles between the sheets. For some reason, he didn't want her to think that he and Candace were a thing.

Deicing to put him out of his misery, she ordered. When the cashier gave them their total, he handed over his card. She tried to slip hers in, but he told her to put it away.

"I don't need you buying my dinner. I have a job; the one you just picked me up from, in fact."

"Do you have to argue about everything?"

She crossed her arms over her chest and gave him an incredulous look. "I don't argue about everything. I'm just stating facts."

"Yes, you do."

Melanie moved to a vacant table to wait. She pulled out her phone as a distraction. He was really getting on her nerves, and she didn't want to talk to him anymore.

Skylar pulled out the seat across from her and sat down. He propped his head in his hands and proceeded to stare at her. Not wanting to give into his games, she kept her eyes on her phone. When she couldn't take it anymore, she set her phone down and mimicked his stance staring him dead in the eyes. They were like two children in the middle of an intense staring contest.

Skylar's name was called and he broke their game to get their order. He didn't know what possessed him to initiate a staring contest with her, but he was finding she gave just as good as she got.

When they got back to their apartment building, he held the front door open for her. They opted to take the elevator instead of the stairs. Skylar hit the button for his floor. Then he stood in front of the buttons blocking her from accessing them.

"What are you doing? Can you hit the button for my floor?"

The elevator reached his floor and he kept looking ahead like he didn't hear her. She placed her foot in between the door and placed her hands on her hips.

"Earth to Skylar! Can I have my stuff? We're on your floor. You can give me mine and I'll head on up."

"No, you can come to my place. I want to try some of what you got too."

"What the heck? You should have ordered some. I want to go to my apartment," she whined.

"Too bad," was all he said.

It dawned on her that she wasn't going to win. Pushing past him out of the elevator, she willed the doors to close on him. She would just let him take what he wanted and then leave. After a day like today, she was ready to have a glass of sparkling grape juice and relax. Wine wasn't her thing, but she felt that sparkling grape juice seemed just as fancy and tasted way better.

Skylar let them into his apartment and headed toward the kitchen. She took in her surroundings as she followed behind him. Their floor plans were identical, but their decorating styles were totally different. His apartment was pretty neat for a bachelor pad. Or at least she thought it was a bachelor pad. Maybe the blonde bombshell lived there. If she did, Melanie wanted to get out of there as fast as possible.

In the kitchen, Skylar retrieved two plates and some utensils. He then grabbed the bag of food and carried them to his living room. She stood in his kitchen looking after him. He returned a moment later and opened his fridge.

"I have water, milk, and some OJ..." He looked over his shoulder at her expecting her to answer.

"Sparkling grape juice. I want sparkling grape juice. In my apartment. On my couch."

"Hmm, I don't have sparkling grape juice so OJ will have to do."

He pulled two glasses from the cabinet and filled them.

"Come on," he said picking up the glasses and heading into his living room.

He'd been dropped on his head as a child. She was sure of it. It was as if he heard nothing she said...ever. What part of her home and sparkling grape juice did the man not understand?

In the living room, he was sitting on the floor with his legs crossed under the coffee table. He was already spooning food onto his plate. Her food at that.

"What the heck, Skylar?"

"What?" He mumbled around a bite of General Tso's Chicken.

"Don't play dumb. You know what."

"I really don't." He wiped the sides of his mouth with a napkin. Maybe he did have manners after all.

"Come sit down, and eat before your food gets cold."

She stood and glared at him. He finally cracked. "Ok, fine. Sometimes I get bored eating alone, and I figured it wouldn't kill us to have a meal together."

"What if I had a date, or plans, or something?" Her hands were placed on her curvy hips.

"Did you?" He popped another bite into his mouth.

"No, but that's beside the point. You can't just bully people into hanging out with you."

"I wouldn't call it bullying. It's more like I surprised you."

A loud laugh bubbled out of her. "A surprise? A freaking surprise? You are terrible at surprises if this is your idea of one."

He smiled at her. *That was the first smile I have seen from him since I met him*, she thought.

"Fine, since you were thoughtful enough to *surprise* me," she made air quotes around the 'surprise', "I guess I can stay."

They ate in comfortable silence while watching a sitcom on T.V. After Melanie had her fill, she decided to start probing for some information.

"So Skylar, what's your last name?"

"That's top secret information. Why do you want to know?"

"I just had dinner with you, so I feel like you at least owe me that. And so I can Facebook-stalk you, of course."

"Dining with a stalker is not a good look for me. Remind me to never have you over for dinner again."

"No worries, I won't fall for your surprises again. So, come on. What is it?"

"Stillman."

"Huh. Not what I was expecting, but it fits."

"What about you?"

"Nova."

"Melanie Nova." She liked the way he said her name, even if she wasn't sure that she liked him. The deep baritone of his voice likely had women's panties dropping in record speed behind closed doors.

"Mr. Stillman, what do you do for a living?"

"I'm a consultant."

"Hmm."

"What's 'hmm' mean?"

"I was trying to decide if I was surprised by that, or not."

"And?"

"I'm not. You try to act quite authoritative with me, so I'm sure you thrive on telling businesses what to do."

"I'm not authoritative with you, and I don't go around just telling businesses what to do."

"Whatever you say."

"Those words sound good coming out of your mouth especially since you are so combative all the time." A smirk was on his face when Melanie looked over at him.

"Well, Mr. Stillman," Melanie moved to get off of the couch. "It's been interesting, but I think it's time to head home."

He made a move to get up as well.

"What time do you need to be at work in the morning?" he asked as he followed her to the door.

She turned her head to look at him over her shoulder.

"I told you that Jade could pick me up. Plus, the tow truck will be here at seven, so I'll already be up and at 'em. No need to bother you with it."

"Yeah, well, I told you and Jade I'd take you in the morning. It's not fair to make her come all the way over here to pick you up when I live right here. So, what time do you need to be there?"

She let out a huff of a breath.

"Ten. I'm only agreeing because I don't want to burden Jade."

"That a girl. Meet you downstairs at 9:30."

CHAPTER FIVE

The next morning, Melanie's alarm went off earlier than usual. She swatted at her phone in an attempt to turn it off. On a normal morning, she set several alarms and hit snooze no less than two times on each before she got up. Mornings weren't her thing. When she was finally able to open her eyes, she saw that it was 6:50 a.m. The tow truck driver would be there soon to get her keys.

Rolling out of bed, she threw on an Indiana University hoodie over the camisole she'd slept in. Yoga pants covered her bottom half. She slipped on a pair of flip-flops and headed out the door. Downstairs, the tow truck was already waiting. There were two men standing outside of it and talking. One of the men had his back facing her. The other was leaning against the truck facing her.

"Hello," she said when she was a few feet from the men. "I'm Melanie. I believe you are here to tow my car."

The man with his back to her turned toward her when he heard her voice.

"What are you doing down here?"

Skylar shrugged one of his shoulders. "Just thought I may be able to be of some help."

He looked at her from head to toe. A ghost of a smile twitched on his lips. What he was thinking? Her hair was on top of her head in a curly mop. Sleep was probably in the corner of her eyes and imprints of her pillow on her face.

"I think I can handle this fine by myself. It doesn't require much to hand over my keys."

"Calm down. I'm just trying to be nice. No need to bite my head off. I'm sure you are perfectly capable." He held his hands up in surrender. She rolled her eyes and turned to the other man. The other man took in their whole exchange and was smiling.

"I'm really sorry about that, sir. Here are my keys. Mine is the blue Honda Accord right there."

Once they figured out what the problem was, they would call and give her an estimate on the cost and how long it would take for the work to be completed. Melanie thanked him and he began the process of loading her car onto the tow truck. Standing by the side walk, she watched as her car was lifted onto the truck. Skylar stood beside her with his hands shoved into the pockets of his sweatpants.

"You don't have to stay out here."

"I know."

They heard the door to the building close and both of them turned to look. The blonde bombshell from a few days ago was walking toward them in a short black skirt, a white button-up blouse and sky-high heels. It looked like Skylar had an eventful night after she left. Her prayers had been answered because she'd slept through it this time. What she couldn't figure out was: if he had a girlfriend, then why did he have her stay for dinner?

The blonde approached Skylar ignoring Melanie altogether. She placed a kiss on his mouth. Melanie did her best to look away and ignore the exchange.

"Hey babe, I have to get to the office. I made a pot of coffee," she said.

"Thanks."

"See you tonight?" Melanie heard the blonde say.

"Probably not. I'm supposed to hang out with Brendon tonight. Guys' night and all."

"Oh, ok. Well, just call me later then."

He must have given her a nod or something in response because Melanie didn't hear him reply. A few minutes later, she was pulling away in her black SUV.

"Exciting night last night, huh?" Melanie asked.

"Something like that."

"You didn't tell me she was your girlfriend last night when we were eating dinner. Did you tell her about that? Because I don't think she would appreciate it too much."

"She isn't my girlfriend, so I don't have to tell her anything."

"Does she know that?"

"Yes, she knows that," Skylar replied in a clipped voice.

"Whatever you say. It's none of my business anyway."

"That's the most sensible thing I've heard you say since I met you."

"I save my good sense for people I like, Mr. Stillman."

* * *

It was a busy day at the boutique and Melanie had several appointments in addition to some walk-ins. Claudia and Jade agreed to dinner later. They needed to catch up, and she wanted to talk to them about her neighbor.

At seven o'clock, Jade and Melanie locked the store up and headed toward a local tapas bar a couple of blocks from the boutique. Claudia was already waiting for them in a booth, sipping on a margarita.

"About time, chicks. This is my second margarita."

"You knew we were coming from work, and you know what time we close," Melanie said. "You just wanted an excuse to drink more."

Claudia narrowed her eyes at Melanie. "Don't act like you know me, li'l girl," she replied, knowing good and well that Melanie knew her better than anyone.

The three of them caught each other up on what had been going on with them. They had a group text that they used to keep up with each other throughout the week, but they used their get-togethers for the juicy stuff.

"Soooo," Melanie drew out.

"Soooo," Claudia replied.

"You guys remember my neighbor, Skylar?"

"Sexy, tall, lean? Yeah, I remember him. That's not a face you forget," said Claudia.

"Agreed," Jade said while nodding her head in confirmation.

"Well, he's given me rides to and from work the last few days since my car broke down. Yesterday, he basically held me hostage at his house for dinner."

Jade's brows lifted in disbelief. "Hostage? Did he hurt you?" she asked, her voice raising an octave.

"No, no, he didn't hurt me. We stopped to get food and, when we got back to the apartment complex, he wouldn't give me mine so I could go home. He made me go to his apartment to eat."

"I hope he ate it off of you," Claudia said with a waggle of her eyebrows.

"No, you perv. He said he doesn't have a girlfriend, but I heard him getting it on with that woman. Then this morning, when my car was being towed, the same girl came out of the building and gave him a kiss before she left."

"Hmm, maybe they are just friends with benefits," Jade offered.

"They are something alright, because the sounds I heard that night were less than pure."

"Maybe you need to offer yourself up to him. You are going through a dry spell. Maybe he can help you out with that," Claudia said while munching on a tortilla chip.

"You are absolutely shameless," Melanie said.

"I call it optimistic."

"Dear Lord," Jade muttered under her breath.

The trio continued to talk and laugh over drinks and tapas. When they were finished, Jade and Melanie hugged Claudia outside of the bar and walked back to Jade's car. Claudia lived within walking distance from the bar, so her margarita indulgence was no problem.

Jade told Melanie that she'd pick her up in the morning. Melanie felt bad burdening her friends, but she knew that, if the shoe was on the other foot, she would do the same. It was nice to finally be rid of Mr. Sourpuss. He liked to boss her around. Think again, dude.

In her apartment, she headed straight for her master bathroom. A nice, long bath and some Netflix was much needed. Tomorrow was Friday, and in her world that meant nothing really. Working in retail meant working weekends which she didn't mind. Those were her best money making days, and they went fast.

The bath bombs made the water bubbly, and she sunk into the warm water. Her tablet sat on the counter with the latest show she'd been watching. Phone in hand, she lazily scrolled through her social media. When she opened up her Facebook, she saw a new friend request and a message. She clicked on the friend request first. Skylar Stillman. His profile picture was of him and his brother dressed up in suits. Brendon had his arm slung over Skylar's shoulders and they looked like they were laughing at something. Both men were handsome, but Skylar was definitely her type.

Before she accepted his friend request, she clicked on the messenger app. Something told her that it was from Mr. Stillman himself. She was correct. The message made her laugh.

Skylar Stillman: To help with your stalking career.

Should she accept his request right away or wait a few days? Her nosiness got the better of her, and she clicked accept. First stop was his wall to see some of his statuses and what people wrote to him. His posts were infrequent.

What really interested her were the pictures. It looked like he lived the life of a bachelor. He had more pictures with his brother. There were some pictures with him, his brother and an older couple that she assumed was their parents. Pictures of him from his college days, and present-day hanging out with his guy friends, were among the others. Oddly enough, he didn't have any pictures alone with the blonde. The few that she was in were taken in a group setting.

Melanie clicked on the blonde's profile and found out her name was Candace. Pictures of her at night clubs and the beach filled her profile. It looked like she lived the life of a socialite.

Melanie was nothing like that. Snuggling up with a good book or Netflix was her idea of fun. She enjoyed some nights on the town with her girls, but only in small doses.

Why was she even comparing herself to this woman? Skylar was her neighbor, nothing more, and she was far from his type. She clicked out of the Facebook app, deciding that she had done enough creeping for one night.

CHAPTER SIX

Jade was there to pick her up at nine-thirty the next morning. Skylar's car was already gone when they were leaving. She figured that was a good thing. Maybe now he would leave her alone about the rides.

The first half of the day was slow, but it picked up in the evening. Everyone was getting ready for the weekend and looking for things to wear. It was early April, and the weather was starting to warm up which meant women were wearing more dresses and bright colors. It was Melanie's favorite time of year both weather and fashion wise.

Midday, the shop called about her car. They advised her that it would be ready on Tuesday, and it was going to set her back about seven hundred dollars. There went a chunk of her savings, but she didn't have much of a choice. Thank goodness the extra income that her blog brought in allowed her to have a little savings.

If she needed to, she could call her dad. He would help her out, but she didn't like to burden him. He had his own life and his own things to worry about. Being a single parent for most of her childhood, he'd provided for her the best he could. She couldn't ask for more than that.

The next few weeks passed in a blur. Things were steady at the boutique, and she'd been busy with taking new pictures for her blog. Companies sometimes sent her things to review and she liked to be as prompt as possible with her posts. With hot new items, her readers wanted the information as quickly as possible so they could make their decision about whether things were worth purchasing.

The boutique had been particularly busy for a Monday. She'd been booked with six appointments that day and had helped with walk-in customers. Her feet were killing her. After taking a quick shower, she whipped up some shrimp stir-fry and parked herself on the couch. A bottle of sparkling grape juice was on hand. Days like today made it mandatory.

Melanie had just forked a mouthful of food into her mouth when there was a knock on the door. She stiffened on the couch for a moment; a little scared. No one stopped by her apartment without calling first. She set her plate down and grabbed the baseball bat she kept around for self-defense. When she looked through the peephole, she let out a sigh of relief. After setting down the bat, she opened the door.

"What are you doing here?"

"Good to see you, too," he replied in a dry tone. "I locked myself out of my apartment."

"Okay. That still doesn't explain why you're *here*. I'm not a locksmith."

"Are you serious? Because I could have sworn your Facebook profile said you were." He said as he held his chin in his hand, like he was really pondering the subject.

"What do you want, Skylar?'

"To hang out on your couch while I wait for my brother."

"Can't you hang out on your girlfriend's couch?"

"No."

"Why not?"

"Because I don't have a girlfriend."

"How long until your brother gets here?"

"About an hour."

"Fine." She walked into the apartment leaving the door open for him to follow.

Settling back on the couch, she pressed play on the remote. He sat down on the other side of the couch.

"Smells good in here."

"Thanks." She kept her eyes focused on the T.V.

"Whatcha eating?"

"Food."

Skylar leaned over to get a glimpse of her plate.

"Sounds delicious. I like food too."

"That's good."

"Aren't you going to share with your poor, homeless neighbor?"

She turned her head slowly to face him. "You are not homeless. You are locked out of your house. The two hardly compare."

He gave her the puppy dog eyes in reply.

"You are insufferable. The food is in the kitchen, and the plates and glasses are in the cabinet. You can serve yourself."

His puppy dog face turned into a full-on grin. She couldn't help but notice how handsome he looked when he smiled like that. She tried not to let it affect her. A few minutes later, he was back with a plate piled with food. So much for leftovers, she thought. He dug into the stir fry and moaned.

"This is so good," he said around a mouthful of food.

"Didn't anyone ever teach you not to talk with your mouth full?"

He swallowed his bite before answering. "Yes, believe it or not, my mom taught me manners. This is really freaking tasty, though."

"Thanks," she said.

They sat in a comfortable silence eating their food and watching Netflix. She didn't know if he'd ever watched the show she was watching before, but he didn't complain about it. When she finished her plate, she pulled the throw that she kept on the back of the couch around her and curled into the corner of the couch.

"You look like you could fall asleep," Skylar said.

"That's because I could. It's been a long day. I'm thankfully off tomorrow though"

"What exactly do you do? I know you work at the boutique, but what do you do?"

"I'm a personal stylist. I basically shop for women. I pick out things that are in style while matching their personal tastes and body shape. They pick pieces they like the best from what I select. I have some everyday clients, and then I have more high profile clients which I make house calls to. I also have a blog on the side."

"Do you like it?"

"Oh, I love it. I've always loved fashion, but I also love making women feel beautiful and confident in their skin. At Finesse & Flare they have clothes for women of all different sizes."

"Are you good at what you do?" Skylar sat back on the couch stretching his feet out in front of him.

"I think so. I'm hoping to branch out and start doing some personal styling on my own as well."

"That would be good; kind of like an entrepreneur."

"That's the goal: to be my own boss one day."

"That's awesome. You have great ambitions."

"What about you? Do you like your job?"

Skylar put one of his hands behind him and rested his head on it.

"I do for the most part. I like going in and fixing problems and helping companies run more efficiently. Not sure it's what I want to do forever, but for now I enjoy it enough."

"What else do you think you would want to do?"

"I'm not really sure yet."

Skylar's phone rang, and he fished it out of his pocket. He rose to his feet while accepting the call.

The call only lasted about thirty seconds.

"Brendon's here, so I guess I'll get out of your hair. Thanks for dinner. If you ever have leftovers, feel free to knock on my door and save me from my endless nights of takeout."

"You're welcome, but I don't know that I'll be providing you with dinner anytime soon."

He walked to the door, and she followed to lock up behind him. Once in the hallway, he gave her a little wave before heading for the elevator.

Back in his apartment, Skylar and his brother decided to play Xbox for a while. They may be grown businessmen, but they still enjoyed a little sibling rivalry by way of video games. His brother left around ten leaving him on the couch watching ESPN. The ring of his phone drew his attention from the T.V. When he looked at the caller ID, he saw that it was Candace. He groaned, knowing that he needed to end things with her. She was getting too clingy even though he'd made it clear that he was not looking for a relationship; a fact that had not changed.

Guaranteed hookups were nice, but he would survive. Better to end it now before she got to 'stage five' clinger status and gave him an ultimatum about a proposal. He hit the answer button. Doing it over the phone would have been easy, but he didn't want to be a complete asshole. Candace asked if she could come over. He agreed, telling her that he needed to talk to her.

While he waited for her, he sipped a beer. He started to wonder if he should have met her in a neutral place. Maybe breaking things off with her in his apartment wasn't his brightest idea. It was too late now though since she was on her way.

A knock sounded at the door. Inhaling a deep breath, he went to let her in. It was now or never. No matter what the head between his legs said he had to deny her advances. He didn't want to have sex with her and then end it. That was too crass even for him.

When he opened the door she was in a skimpy outfit that didn't cover much of her body. It was spring time, but the evenings were still cool. Small arms wrapped around his neck and pulled him down for a kiss before he had time to protest. A sultry smile played on her face when she pulled away. He knew what that smile meant, but he wasn't going to give in. Their thing had run its course and it was time for both of them to move on.

"Hey," he stepped back out of her embrace. She looked a little confused for a moment. "We need to talk. Let's go have a seat on the couch."

Candace picked her seat and Skylar sat down making sure to leave a space between them.

"What's going on?" she asked with worry laced in her tone.

"When we started this, we both knew it was casual. I never wanted anything serious; just some fun and companionship. I think that it is time that we go our separate ways. I'm afraid things may be getting too complicated."

Candace's face fell. Tears welled in her eyes. *Oh shit*, he thought to himself. Things were worse than he thought.

"Don't cry, Candace. I'm really sorry. I was trying to do the right thing by ending it before feelings got involved."

"But I- I think I love you, Skylar. I thought that we were moving forward. I thought that you were past the 'just hooking up' stage." She wiped at her eyes with her finger.

"I'm so sorry, Candace. I don't feel the same way. If I had realized your feelings were changing, I would have ended things sooner. The last thing I wanted to do was hurt you."

She reached her hand out and grasped his in hers.

"Maybe you just need time. Maybe we can take a break and you can think about if you want a relationship," she sniffled.

Skylar peeled her hand from his with his free hand.

"I don't think my mind will change, Candace. I'm sorry."

She picked up her purse and stormed to the door.

"You will miss me, Skylar. When you realize that, you better hope I haven't moved on."

She didn't wait for him to see her out she just slammed the door behind her. Skylar fell back onto the couch. What an absolute mess he had caused. The 'L' word was brought up. Skylar did not have time for women to be falling in love with him. He didn't have anything more than sex to offer to a woman. If he *ever* settled down, he was a long way away from that day. Even if he wasn't, he didn't think Candace would be the woman for him.

CHAPTER SEVEN

After working on her latest blog post, Melanie decided to take a break. She was sitting out on her patio enjoying a book when her phone rang.

"Hey, old man. How are you?"

"I'm good, sweetheart. How's my girl?"

Phone calls with her dad always made her happy. He had moved to Texas a few years ago after he married his wife, Gwen, and Melanie missed him.

"I'm good, pops. Just working and trying to grow my blog."

"That's my girl; always working hard. I hope you're taking care of yourself too."

"I am. How's Gwen?"

"She's good. She's been busy tending to the garden. When are you coming to visit us?"

It never failed. Her dad always asked the same question. She missed her dad, but she had a job that was hard to get away from for too long. Never mind the travel expenses.

"You know I'll pay for your plane ticket, and you can stay here for free."

"I know, Dad. Hopefully I'll be able to come soon."

"Alright, sweetheart. I love you."

"I love you too, Dad."

The call ended and Melanie stared out into evening sky thinking about her dad.

"Where are you going soon?" She looked down over her railing and saw Skylar looking back up at her.

"Eavesdropping on people's conversations now?"

"I wouldn't call it eavesdropping since you were having said conversation in public, and I just happened to be on my patio."

She stuck her tongue out at him.

"Very mature, Mel."

"I learned from the best," she countered.

"What are you up to?"

"Enjoying this weather and the last bit of my day off."

"Want to come down and hang with me and Brendon?"

"Why would I want to do that?" Her eyebrows rose.

He scoffed at that. "Why wouldn't you want to do that?"

She put her finger on her chin as if she were really pondering this question.

"First off, you don't even like me. Second, you don't really know me. Shall I keep going?"

"I never said I didn't like you, and I know you well enough."

"You didn't have to. Ever hear the saying 'actions speak louder than words'?"

Brushing her words off, Skylar pressed on.

"Well, we have pizza and brownies if you want to come down."

"Sounds like girls' night to me."

"We are men; manly men at that. We just like baked goods. As a matter of fact, when you start to bring me dinner, you can bring me some baked goods as well. Come down or don't; suit yourself."

Skylar disappeared through his sliding glass door, and Melanie was left to her own peace and quiet. She'd been debating what to do for dinner. T.V. dinner or takeout were the options. With it being her day off, she didn't feel like cooking anything.

Going to Skylar's would be a bad idea, but why should she pay for food when he'd already done so? She could put up with him long enough for a free meal, and then she'd be out. With that decided she went into her apartment, poured a glass of sparkling grape juice and headed out the door.

Less than a minute later, she was knocking on his front door. The sounds of a muffled T.V. and footsteps came from behind the door. Skylar swung the door open.

"We've been expecting you."

"I never said I was coming." Melanie fought to keep the smile off of her face.

"You didn't have to. No one turns down fresh brownies."

"Was that a fat joke?"

Skylar's mouth dropped open and he was momentarily at a loss for words.

"Why the hell would that be a fat joke?"

"Don't play dumb," she said and gestured to her body. "Clearly I don't have the body of a model."

"I-I would never say something like that to you or any other woman. You look fine to me. I was simply stating that everyone likes brownies. And if they don't, they aren't human."

Melanie studied him for a second trying to decide if he was being genuine. She didn't see any malice in his expression. Her hunched shoulders relaxed while she moved further into the apartment. Brendon was in the living room shoving half a slice of pizza into his mouth. When he spotted her walking in, he patted the spot next to him with his free hand.

"Hey, pretty lady, come sit by me."

"Aren't you just the charmer?" she laughed as she made her way over to him.

Brendon looked over his shoulder at his brother. "Get the lady a plate, would ya? Don't you have any manners?" He playfully nudged Melanie in her side like they were in cahoots.

Skylar turned toward the kitchen while mumbling under his breath. When he came back, he handed her a plate and some napkins.

"Take whatever you like," he told her. "I would offer you a drink, but it looks like you already have one. Wine?"

"Nope, it's sparkling grape juice. It's my kryptonite. Not much of a drinker."

"Is that so?"

"Yep, and you'll know why if you ever get the displeasure of seeing me drunk."

Brendon snickered beside her. "I know my new mission in life."

Melanie rolled her eyes and added two pieces of Hawaiian pizza to her plate. She tucked her feet under her and cuddled into the couch. The three of them sat and watched a reality T.V. show and chatted about who would be voted off and who should win.

"So, bro, you still seeing Candace?"

Skylar glanced at Melanie before answering his brother. Why his brother picked the worst times to bring things up, he did not know. Although he wasn't sure why he cared what Melanie thought about his love life. He didn't like her like that. They weren't even quite friends.

"I wasn't really seeing her like that, but nah, things are done."

"What happened?"

Skylar could tell that Melanie was eager to hear what he said too. She tried to act like she wasn't that interested, but it wasn't working.

"She was starting to get clingy, and I could tell she forgot that it was never supposed to be serious. I broke it off before she could get hurt."

"Had a clinger huh, bro?"

"Something like that."

Brendon stretched his arm out and rested it behind Melanie on the couch.

"So Mel, what's your story?"

Melanie laughed to herself at how familiar Brendon was; using her nickname and resting his arm behind her tickled her. He was a jokester and she liked him already.

"There isn't much to me really."

"Ah come on, a cutie like you has got to have something to say. Are you from here? What do you do? What makes you hot?"

A loud laugh burst from Melanie. "You are something else," she said when she caught her breath.

"I'm from a small town in central Indiana. I'm a personal stylist. I also run my own fashion blog. As for what makes me hot, I can't just give out that kind of top secret information."

Brendon laughed, "Fair enough."

"What about you?"

"I'm a nerd."

"Oh, really? That's your official title?"

"Pretty much. I've created a few start-up technology companies that I sold early on. I still own one; it's my baby. I like all things computers and developing. My bank account would say I'm pretty good at it too." He took a swig from his beer.

"And you don't lack confidence either. Pretty impressive."

The two of them continued to talk about random things. Skylar was pretty quiet; only contributing to the conversation every so often. Melanie caught him staring at her once, but she assumed he was a bit buzzed from the beer.

Brendon finally made his move to leave. He and Melanie exchanged phone numbers and hugged like they were old friends. Once he was out the door, Melanie started to clean up.

"What are you doing?"

"Cleaning up some of the mess we made."

"You don't have to do that. I'll get it."

"It's rude to go to someone's house and not offer to help clean up, Skylar. Plus, I don't mind."

She carried the dishes into the kitchen and began to wash them by hand. Skylar came up beside her and rinsed them before putting them on the drying rack.

"So you and Brendon got along well."

Melanie chuckled lightly. "Yeah, he seems like a really nice guy. He is goofy."

"He's definitely that."

"Is he your only sibling, or do you have more?"

"We have one sister. She's the baby of the bunch. She's getting married in a few weeks."

"Oh, my goodness, that's so exciting! Does she live here? Where is the wedding?"

"Yes, she lives here. The wedding is going to be at our parent's house. They have a nice sized piece of land. She wanted something intimate."

"I bet her wedding is going to be magical. You have to show me some pictures."

"I'll see what I can do. I'm sure I'll be tagged in a bunch of photos I don't want to take on Facebook."

"What's your family like? Is everyone goofy like Brendon or serious like you?"

"Hey, I can be goofy. I just take life a little more seriously than Brendon. He's sitting on a nice chunk of change, so he can afford to be crazy. Technology stuff comes easy to him which means money does too."

"Well, he certainly doesn't act like a stuck-up rich guy. He's very fun and nice."

"Yeah, he'll give you the shirt off his back. He's paying for our sister Sam's wedding."

"Wow, he just keeps amazing me."

Skylar resisted an eye roll.

"Anywho, tell me about Sam and your parents."

"Sam is the youngest like I said. We were super protective of her as a kid. She always wanted to hang out with us and do boy stuff. We let her tag along mostly because mom made us, but she has tough skin now because of it. She doesn't take any crap from anyone. She's a little thing, kind of like you, but she's feisty. She'll call you on your bullshit in a heartbeat. Got a heart of gold though. If she loves you, she will do anything for you."

Melanie could hear the love that he had for his sister when he talked about her. It was precious how much he adored her.

"Mom and Dad are great, too. Mom is an artist. She paints and makes jewelry. She's very eclectic. She recently got into running those wine and canvas type of classes, so she stays busy. Dad's a teacher at the local high school and helps coach the cross country team. He loves being around the kids; says it helps keep him young."

"Your parents sound lovely. So does Sam. So, what happened to you?"

Skylar put his hand over his chest in mock offense.

"Hey, I invited you down for pizza and brownies. I'm a very nice guy."

"I suppose you have done some nice things for me since we met. You are just so bossy and hostile looking sometimes. The first time I met you, I thought you wanted to do some bodily harm."

"Yeah, I was pretty irritated. I won't lie. You seem alright, though. Hardheaded maybe, but you're ok."

She put on her best southern bell accent. "Well, I do declare. I have never received such a flattering compliment in all my life." She battered her eyelashes for added effect.

"Add smart aleck to that description." He rolled his eyes. "Tell me about your family."

"Not much to tell. My mom died when I was ten. It was me and my dad from then on out. He did his best to raise me. He came to all the school plays, cooked dinner, we went on vacations… He is the absolute best."

The smile on her face was big as she spoke about her dad.

"What does he do for a living?"

"He works at a bank. He's worked his way up to some prestigious position. I don't even know what exactly to be honest. Let's just say he is a big deal at his bank."

"Tell me about your mom."

She had no idea why she was considering talking to him about her mother. Melanie didn't know why she was telling him anything about her life at all. They weren't friends; she barely knew him. But, for some reason, she felt comfortable talking to him. Maybe it was the sincerity in his inquiries. Maybe because, instead of having the look of pity in his eyes, he actually asked about her mother.

"She was beautiful. I know most people would say that about their mother, but she really was beautiful inside and out. We used to have pamper days. We'd get our nails done and have tea time. She worked at a halfway home that helped people get back on their feet after being on drugs. Her heart was kind and she had a need to change the world, and that she did."

"She sounds amazing, Mel."

"She was."

"If you don't mind me asking: what happened to her?"

"She had kidney failure."

Melanie felt the all too familiar lump forming in the back of her throat.

"I bet you still miss her."

It seemed weird, but she was thankful he didn't offer the standard condolences, yet he still recognized that it was life changing.

"Yes, very much." She let the water out of the sink and wiped her hands on a nearby towel. "I better get going. I have to work in the morning. Thanks for dinner."

"No problem. I'm hoping that this means I may get an invite to one of your homemade meals."

"We'll see about that. I suppose you do deserve a little something for your troubles."

He fist pumped the air. "Yessss," he hissed out.

"You act like it's a done deal," she laughed.

"I can tell you're a nice girl, so it's totally happening."

She shook her head and opened the front door. "Bye, Skylar."

"Bye, Mel."

CHAPTER EIGHT

"Guys, I think I want to join Tinder," Melanie said while sipping juice on her couch a few nights later.

"About dang time," Claudia replied. "You haven't been laid in like eighty-seven years."

"Hardy-har-har, smarty pants. I'm not just looking for a hookup. I think I may want something more serious; at least a friend with benefits that I can cuddle with sometimes."

"Maybe you should try something besides Tinder," Jade suggested.

"Like what?"

"Maybe one with a membership? They seem legit."

"Those sites take your money just to do the same stuff all the other sites do," Claudia protested. "Try the freebies out first. I'm sure a lot of these people have accounts on multiple sites."

Melanie let out a huff. "Why can't meeting someone be easy? The Internet has made it easier and harder at the same time. It feels like the only way is online dating and, with that, you never know what you'll get. Add in being plus-size and it's like a war out there."

Claudia and Jade nodded in agreement.

"All I know, " Claudia said, "is we are all fine as heck, and whatever men snag us will be lucky S.O.Bs."

"Cheers to that," Jade raised her glass.

"What are you waiting for? Download the app and let's get this party started!" Claudia squealed.

That following Friday, Mel stood in front of her bathroom mirror putting on the final touches of makeup. Any minute, her first online dating excursion was set to begin. She was meeting him at a local pub for dinner and drinks. There was no way she was giving out her address to a stranger. Her stomach was full of butterflies and her mind full of doubt.

Claudia and Jade helped her pick out the perfect first date outfit. Claudia said it was flirty with a bit of 'come-and-get-it' sexy; whatever that meant. She knew she looked fine, but she hadn't been on a date in months. She'd resigned herself to being a crazy goldfish lady. Not caring much for cats, goldfish seemed like a simpler alternative.

With one last look in her full-length mirror, she had a little panic attack. Her breathing became labored and she felt dizzy. She sat on the side of her bed and took several deep breaths. When she was calm enough, she grabbed her clutch and left. In her car, she hooked her phone to Bluetooth and three way called Claudia and Jade.

"Aren't you supposed to be on a date?" was Claudia's greeting.

"I'm freaking the hell out. What if I don't look like my pictures? What if he thinks I "catfished" him?" Her voice raised and her words ran together.

"Calm down, you nut. You look exactly like your pictures, and you better hope he isn't catfishing you."

Jade cut Claudia off.

"Claudia, you are not helping things! Mel, it's only one date. It isn't marriage. It will be fine. If you don't have chemistry, you don't have to meet again. No harm, no foul."

"OK, I can do this. It will be fine."

"That's right and, just remember, he is a lucky guy to get the privilege of spending the evening with you. Call us when you get home, ok?"

"Ok, Mom," Melanie said with a laugh.

Jade was the calm and sane one of their group. She was always the voice of reason. Melanie was thankful for her. Claudia was a bit of a wild child at times, and Jade reeled them back into sanity. She loved them both dearly.

Melanie stood outside of the pub taking a few calming breaths. She looked at her phone and found a text from Garrett, the man she was meeting that night.

Garrett: Hey, just wanted to let you know I'm here. I'm at the front as soon as you walk in.

She didn't bother with replying. She swung the door open before giving herself time to overthink. She recognized him immediately. He was wearing nice, dark washed jeans and a button down shirt. The sleeves were rolled up halfway exposing his forearms. He looked like his pictures, although he was shorter than she expected. That was ok, she told herself, because she was short too. Most men towered over her. Their eyes locked and it seemed like he recognized her as well. His eyes did a perusal of her face and body as he walked toward her.

When he was close enough, he began to speak. "You must be Melanie."

"Yes, I am. So that must make you Garrett."

He went in for a small hug. Melanie felt awkward, but she didn't want to be rude so she returned the hug with a one-armed, slight tap on the back. When they released, he smiled at her. She smiled back not knowing what else to do.

"Let's see about getting our table," Garrett said and gestured toward the hostess stand.

The hostess led them to a dimly lit booth toward the back of the restaurant. It seemed like the perfect table for an intimate date, but Melanie wasn't so sure that fit the bill for this outing. She started to question why she hadn't insisted on meeting for coffee or something during the day. It was too late to second guess her decision, so she slid into the booth. She was sure she was overreacting. It had been a long time since she had been on a date, and she had never been on a date that had been initiated from an online dating site. People did it all the time, so it couldn't be that bad.

"So, Melanie, tell me more about yourself."

They had exchanged a few text messages since they met through the app, but they hadn't gone too in-depth. She wasn't sure how much she should reveal about her life. Since it was the first date, she decided to stick to the basics.

"Well, I was born and raised here. I'm a Hoosier girl through and through. I work at a local boutique as a personal stylist. I help women find clothes for all occasions from honeymoons and formal events to everyday wardrobes. What about you?"

"I'm actually from Tennessee and moved here for a job. I work as an account manager. I went to school for business and had a focus in marketing. I do some marketing work with up-and-coming entrepreneurs on the side."

"That's really awesome. I'm hoping to be an entrepreneur one day. I have a blog and I hope to branch out and build my own clientele that I do personal shopping for."

"I like a woman that has ambition. If you put in the work, you will make it happen. I'm sure of it."

She offered him a shy smile. "I hope you're right."

Their conversation shifted to things like favorite music, hobbies, and movies. They had a common interest in comedies. They also liked some of the same music. As they worked their way through dinner and to dessert, Melanie thought that things were going really well.

When the waiter came to see if they wanted dessert, Garrett ordered his and insisted that she order one as well. She ordered a chocolate lava cake a la mode. If he insisted, then who was she to deny?

Melanie took a bite of her cake. A moan of delight threatened to escape. Her eyes flicked to Garrett who was staring at her with what she thought was a look of lust. It made her feel a little self-conscious.

"Did you want to try a bite? It's really good."

"No, you go ahead," he said. Clearing his throat, he spoke again. "This may be weird, but can I feed you?"

Melanie choked on the sip of water she'd taken. "Um." She was not sure how to respond. Her mind said *'Hell no, creep'*, but she didn't want to be rude. "I don't know if that would be a good idea. We're in the middle of the restaurant and this is our first date. I'm sorry."

She tried to smile but it looked more like a grimace.

"It's ok. I know that may have come off a bit weird. It's just that you are so beautiful. I love your body, and the look on your face when you had the first bite was so sexy."

If Melanie could blush, her face would be as red as a tomato.

"Thank you?"

"You're welcome. I'm hoping we can go out again after this. I love seeing a woman of your stature enjoying delicious food." He was smiling at her like it was the most natural thing in the world to say.

"A woman of my stature?"

"Yeah, plus-size women. You are so infatuating."

"Oookay."

"I hope I'm not being too forward. When I saw your profile, I thought you were perfect."

Melanie had nothing. She was beginning to realize what was going on. Garrett had a fetish. What.The.Heck. Getting out of there turned into her top priority. Being polite and hurrying this along seemed her best bet.

"Thank you, Garrett. You are very...sweet."

The server brought their bill and a sense of relief fell over Melanie. Just a few more minutes and she could make her escape. He grabbed the check and slid his card into the black booklet. A few minutes later the server picked it up.

"Would you like to go somewhere to have drinks? We could go to my place and have some wine."

"Oh, I have to work in the morning. I really should get home."

"It's a bummer that you have to work on the weekends."

"I don't mind it. I love my job. If I really need time off, my boss is great about letting me have it."

Melanie's eyes scanned the restaurant for their server.

"Maybe you can take next weekend off and we can spend a little more time together."

Where the hell was the server with their check? She couldn't take much more of this nutcase. She wanted to go home, pour herself some sparkling grape juice and relax in a bubble bath. This online dating thing was for the birds. B.O.B would have to continue taking care of her needs for the time being. Companionship was overrated. That's what romance novels were for, and she could live vicariously through romance novels with her fish.

Finally, the server came back with their check. The woman thanked them for dining there, and then she was gone. Melanie decided it was now or never. She pulled her purse onto her shoulder.

"Thank you so much for tonight. I had better get going."

"I really wish you could go for drinks, but I understand; duty calls."

She managed a fake laugh. "Yep, duty calls."

She stood up from her seat and he followed suit. He placed his hand on the small of her back and began to guide her toward the door. It felt like his hand was burning a hole in her back, and not in a good way. Just a few short minutes and she would be home free.

Garrett walked her all the way to her car. When she turned back around to tell him goodbye, he was only a few inches from her face. His hands rested on her hips while she leaned away from him back into the car.

"I had a really nice time with you tonight, Melanie. You are a beautiful woman, and I would really like to see you again."

"I'm not sure when I'll be available again. Things are pretty busy with work and my blog."

"Surely you can find a little time for a friend?"

"Uh, maybe. We'll see." She saw a flash of confusion in his face, but he didn't let that deter him.

"Ok, well; I'll text you, and hopefully we can work something out."

"Sounds good."

Before he could try to make a move, Melanie got into her car and drove away. When she looked back, she saw him standing with his hands in his pockets. She felt bad because he seemed like a really nice guy, but she was not going to be someone's fetish. She had spent too many years learning to love herself, and she wasn't about to let anyone objectify her. It didn't matter how nice he seemed.

CHAPTER NINE

When Melanie finally turned the ignition off in front of her apartment, she was relieved. She was headed to the front door when she heard her name being called. Her back stiffened for a moment, and instinct told her to keep walking until she was inside of the well-lit building.

"Mel, wait up."

Against her better judgment, she turned around. The tension immediately left her body. It was Skylar who was walking toward her with a takeout bag.

"Hey, what are you up to?" he asked.

"Just got home from the world's worst date."

"The worst date ever, huh? It had to be pretty epic to be the worst."

"Epic is not the word I would use for it." As they reached the front door, Skylar held it open and let her walk in first. When the elevator arrived, Melanie pushed the buttons for their respective floors. When they reached his floor, he pressed the button to close the doors.

"What are you doing? This is your floor."

"I know, but I want to hear about the world's worst date."

"I don't think so."

"Why not? You seem upset. You obviously want to talk about it."

She folded her arms across her chest. Discussing her disastrous date with Skylar was not on top of her list of things to do. How could he ever understand? He was handsome and had an ideal body. Women probably approached him on the daily. Women probably never said 'no' to him. Talking to him about this would be humiliating.

"Come on, Mel. I'm a good listener."

"I bet you are," she said with an eye roll.

"I am."

The door opened to her floor, and he headed off of the elevator in front of her. When she exited, he was already standing by her front door.

"You are a pest, you know that?"

"Hey, I'm just trying to be a friend. I'll even share my dinner if you'd like."

"No, thanks; the date from hell included dinner."

"If he took you to dinner, it couldn't have been that bad. Did he make you pay or something?"

"No."

Melanie kicked her heels off at the door and went into the kitchen. She pulled a plate from the kitchen cabinet and set it on the counter for Skylar. She pulled out a wine glass for herself and filled it to the brim with sparkling grape juice. She disappeared into her room. When she reappeared, she'd changed into leggings and a hoodie. Her feet were covered in some SpongeBob slippers.

"What are those?" Skylar pointed to her feet.

"What do they look like?"

"SpongeBob slippers?"

"Ding, ding, ding! You win whatever is behind door number one!"

"You're a smarty pants, aren't you?"

"It's one of my strong suits."

Skylar had put the contents of his takeout bag on the plate she set out for him. He'd also helped himself to a bottle of water from her fridge. Perched in the corner of her couch, he devoured his burger and fries.

He swallowed the last bite and wiped his mouth with a napkin.

"Come on, tell me what happened."

She sighed and took a long drink of her juice. She didn't want to tell him, but she knew that she was going to.

"It's embarrassing. You have to promise not to laugh."

"How can I promise when I don't know what you're going to say? If he was a real tool, I may find some humor in his ignorance." She glared over at him. "Fine, ok. I promise."

"We went to a nice restaurant. Things were going well. We had some things in common, and the conversation was flowing. Dinner came, and then he insisted I get dessert." Skylar nodded his head to encourage her to keep going.

Mel took a big gulp of air and closed her eyes before proceeding.

"When our dessert came, he asked me if he could... feed me."

"What the hell? Why would he ask you that? How well do you know this guy?"

Melanie cracked her eye open. She was relieved that he didn't laugh like she'd half expected him to.

"This was our first time meeting in person. We met on one of those dating apps."

"That's a creepy request. What did you say?"

"I told him that it wasn't a good idea since we were in a public place, and it was our first date!"

"Did he say why he wanted to feed you? Was he trying to seduce you?"

"He said that he was attracted to girls of my 'stature'," she used air quotes. "Plus-size women infatuate him. When he saw my profile, he knew I was perfect. Basically, he has a fat girl fetish."

Taking the blanket from the back of her couch, she covered her head with it. She could not believe that she'd told this to Skylar. He was going to look at her differently. Not that he knew her well enough to have much to go off of to begin with.

"What a douche. You don't need someone like him."

"Yeah."

"I'm serious, Melanie. You can do way better. You have to have guys hitting on you all the time. You don't need a dating app full of weirdos with fetishes."

"Gosh, I was so stupid. I don't know why I thought I would be able to find someone who would see me for me. This is exactly why I don't date. It's too much effort for a whole lot of grief."

"Mel, don't beat yourself up because one dude was a dud. You are a beautiful woman. I'm sure many men want your body for all the right reasons, but more importantly; they will be intrigued by your mind. I don't know you that well yet, but I can tell what kind of person you are. Don't settle for just any guy. Make sure he treats you like you deserve to be treated."

Melanie was a little shocked by Skylar's words. He said she was beautiful. That didn't matter though. Skylar was just being nice and trying to cheer her up. It was kind of working.

"Thanks, Skylar, but I think I'm going to be off the dating scene for a while. I might swear off online dating forever."

"Don't give up. There is someone out there. He will probably turn up when you aren't looking; when you least expect it."

"I doubt it, but I'll take your word for it."

They sat in silence for a bit watching some show that was on the T.V. Oddly it wasn't an uncomfortable silence. Melanie was comfortable with his presence. She wasn't sure why because she didn't have a lot of male friends, and she definitely didn't have men over to her home - like, ever. Even though she and Skylar had started off rocky, he seemed like an ok guy. He listened to her dating woes, and that had to count for something even if it was embarrassing to admit to someone like him.

"Hey," Skylar startled her from her own thoughts. "My parents are having a barbecue next week. It will be family and friends. They have a pool and a nice sound system, so it's usually a good time. You should come."

That was not what she was expecting to hear. She could use a little poolside relaxation, but she didn't know how much she could really relax around a bunch of strangers. Being shy wasn't in her nature. It couldn't be in her line of work. Thanks to her love for fashion, she had some banging suits to wear; she was still unsure.

"I don't know, Skylar. I don't want to intrude on your family's gathering."

"You wouldn't be intruding. It's family and friends, and we are friends aren't we? I mean I've fed you. You've fed me. If that isn't friendship, I don't know what is."

She had to laugh at that. "When you put it like that, I suppose we may be becoming friends."

"See, so you have no reason not to come. My family will love you. You don't take any of my crap."

"And don't you forget it," she said with a playful tone.

"So that's a yes then? You can just ride with me. It's Saturday, and we can leave at noon. It takes about an hour to get to my folks' house."

"How do you know that is a yes? What if I have to work?"

"Do you?"
"Well, no. But..."
"No 'buts', you're going."

* * *

It was eleven thirty on Saturday, and Melanie was standing in front of the mirror debating what to wear. She decided to wear her bathing suit under whatever she chose. A bright pink beach bag was filled with poolside essentials. Her e-reader had several beach reads downloaded and ready. Despite it being a party, she thought she may get a few moments of solitude.

She always struggled with clothing for things like this. It was heightened by the fact that she only knew two people that were going to be there. In her eyes, her outfits were personal reflection of her brand. Her life revolved around fashion. Every social opportunity had the potential to turn into a business opportunity.

Since it was casual, she decided on a pair of black shorts with lace detailing. On top was a light-weight, off the shoulder top in yellow. Yellow looked great on her brown skin. She kept her shoes simple as well.

Ten minutes later, she heard a knock on her door. She knew it had to be Skylar. No one else knocked on her door unannounced except Claudia, and she knew that Melanie was going to be gone. Why was he early, though? Didn't he know that women needed up to the last second to get ready? She headed to the door and checked the peephole to confirm it was him.

He was standing there in cargo shorts, a tank top with some logo on it, and flip-flops. Sunglasses were perched on the top of his head. He knocked again, and she pulled back from the peephole. She needed to stop being a peeping Tom and open the door. Not wanting him to know she'd been standing there staring, she waited a few seconds to open the door.

"You're early."
"Good day to you, too, SpongeBob."
She rolled her eyes at him. "Stop calling me that."
"Why? Your slippers are adorable."
Adorable is not what she wanted a man like Skylar to call her. Maybe temptress or vixen. She'd settle for beautiful or pretty.

"I was bored, so I decided to come up. Don't let me interrupt. You can finish getting ready."

"Thank you so much, Skylar."

She gave him a fake smile and walked into her bedroom. In her bathroom, she checked the mirror one last time. When she went back into her bedroom, Skylar was perched on the edge of her bed looking at a picture of Melanie and her dad.

"What are you doing in my bedroom?"

He had the nerve to look confused by her question. "Um, waiting on you to be ready to go. Is this your dad?"

"You could have done that in the living room. I didn't invite you in here. Yes, that's him."

"You didn't not invite me either."

"You are impossible." She picked up her bag off of the bed and headed toward her bedroom door.

"Come on, get out of my room. I'm ready to go."

They headed out to Skylar's car. He walked toward the passenger side door. She wondered what he was doing, but figured maybe he needed to move some things out of the seat. When he reached the door, he opened it and motioned for her to get in. He waited for her to get situated before he shut the door and went around to the driver side. Maybe he did have manners.

She glanced over at him as he started the car and eased out of his parking space. This wasn't anything formal, but she was still nervous to meet his family. Brendon and her clicked immediately, and she loved him. Fingers crossed the rest of his family were as nice and easy-going as him. They couldn't be stuck up if they raised someone like Brendon. When Skylar described them, they sounded like nice people.

She was also worried about meeting their family friends. The fear of other's judgment was always in the back of her mind no matter how far she'd come in accepting and loving the skin she was in. Not everyone was as open minded as others. Oh well, who did she need to impress? She and Skylar were just friends.

CHAPTER TEN

They rode in silence for most of the ride. About thirty minutes into the drive, Skylar glanced over at her.

"Why so quiet? You nervous?"

She took a moment before she answered. "No...Yes. A little."

"Why are you nervous? You know Brendon and me. The rest of my family is nice. Nicer than me, and you hate me, so it can only go up from here."

She deadpanned over to him. "Well, if they're nicer than you, I'll be fine."

He chuckled at her sarcasm. "I can't be that bad because you agreed to come today."

"I like swimming, and Brendon."

"You sure know how to inflate a guy's ego."

They passed the rest of the car ride in silence. Light music played over the radio. She assumed the mix came from his phone because several genres played throughout the ride. They had a lot more in common music-wise than she would have imagined.

Skylar's parents lived in a secluded country area. A two-story house painted in a light blue with white trim came into view. Melanie's mouth dropped open. There was a wraparound porch that matched the white of the trim. Flowerbeds lined the front of the porch, and a swing hung to the left of the front door. It was beautiful. The home seemed to be sitting on many acres of land. She felt a sense of peace surround her.

Skylar put the car in park and came around to her side before she could get her seatbelt off. He opened the door and held his hand out to help her out of the car. She stared at his hand for a moment. Torn between taking it and being gracious or ignoring it and getting out on her own, she opted to ignore it. Any unnecessary physical contact with him was best to avoid.

A smirk played on his lips when she emerged, but she ignored it. He grabbed her bag from her hand and led the way to the house. A few cars already lined the driveway when they arrived. Skylar opened the door without knocking and led them into a beautiful foyer. They walked down a hall lined with pictures that had to be of Skylar and his family over the years.

He led her into the kitchen where a few women busied themselves.

"Hey ladies," Skylar said into the room.

All the women turned to see who the voice belonged to. A woman who looked to be in her mid-twenties ran and flung herself at Skylar. Her black hair was cut into a short bob. Big green eyes stared up at him. She was short, maybe five feet. Skylar caught the woman and swung her around before setting her down.

"Hey, Sammie, it's good to see you too." He tousled her hair. She smacked him on the shoulder.

"What have I told you about touching my hair? I'm not five anymore," the woman, who Melanie now knew was his sister Sam, said.

An older woman that was almost an identical version of Sam came over and gave Skylar a hug. Her black hair was peppered with some gray. She had eyes a shade lighter than Sam's, and they had lines around them as if she laughed often.

"Hey, my sweet boy. I'm so happy to see you." When she pulled away she looked in Melanie's direction. "Who is this lovely girl here, Sky?"

Skylar turned toward Melanie and placed his hand on her lower back pushing her forward.

"Mom, this is my neighbor, Melanie. Melanie, this is my mom, Arabella, and my sister, Sam."

Melanie smiled and put her hand out to shake his mother's.

"It's so nice to meet you, Mrs. Stillman."

To her surprise, Mrs. Stillman bypassed the hand and pulled her in for a quick hug.

"Please, call me Arabella, dear. Mrs. Stillman is far too formal." When she released her from the hug, she said, "Neighbor, huh?" and looked at her son with a small smile. He acted like he didn't see it.

Sam was next to pull Melanie into a hug. "It's so good to meet you, Melanie. Can I call you Mel? I've heard so much about you. It's nice to put a face to the name."

She'd heard about her? What had Skylar told his family about her? Did they know that she didn't like him, or used to dislike him? She was coming around now. Melanie gave Sam a shy smile.

"It's nice to meet you too."

"Ok, guys, enough smothering Mel; we're going out back. We'll see you in a bit."

Melanie gave Skylar's mother and sister a small wave as she followed him. She happened to look back over her shoulder to shut the screen door, and she saw the two women with their heads together conspiring about something.

When they got outside, Skylar headed over to the grill; a man was tending to the food. He was a little shorter than Skylar and had light brown hair. He had a mustache, and glasses were perched on his face.

"Hey, Pops." Skylar slapped the older man on his back.

"Hey, Sky. Good to see you." The man turned around and did the one-armed man hug with his son.

Skylar turned toward Melanie and introduced her to his father.

"Nice to meet you, young lady."

"Nice to meet you too, sir."

"Call me Wallace."

She smiled up at the older man. "Ok, Wallace."

Suddenly, she felt strong arms snake around her from behind and she was being lifted into the air. She let out a little screech.

"Hey, good lookin," the familiar voice said in her ear as he set her back on the ground. When she turned, around Brendon had a big smile on his face.

"Brendon, you goon. You scared me half to death!"

He laughed at her admonishment. "What can I say? I like to sweep beautiful ladies off of their feet."

She couldn't help but smile at his silly antics. The pair had hit it off, and Melanie knew that he was a goofball. That was why she liked him so well. When she looked over at Skylar, he had a weird look on his face. He quickly replaced it with a smile once he caught her gaze. She thought it was kind of weird, but let it slide. He was the more serious of the brothers and she chalked it up to that.

"You swimming today, darlin'?" Brendon asked her.

"I brought my suit, so I hope to."

"We are going to play some pool games if you want to go change into your bathing suit."

Sam walked up to their little group.

"Sounds like fun," Melanie said.

"Hey, Sam, can you show Melanie where she can change into her suit. We're getting ready to get in the pool."

"Of course I can," Sam replied and reached for Melanie's hand before pulling her toward the house.

They were only a few feet away when Brendon yelled after them, "Need any help getting ready?"

Melanie stuck her tongue out at him and saw that Skylar hit him upside the back of his head. That didn't faze Brendon; he just laughed it off.

As Sam was leading her to the bathroom, she flooded her with questions.

"Where did you meet Skylar?"

"It's kind of funny. My friends and I were having a girls' night, and Skylar came banging on my door. He and Brendon were watching some ballgame, and he said we were being too loud. I tried to offer him pizza, but he wasn't too receptive to my charm." Melanie chuckled remembering how gruff he had been the first night. "Your brother is easily ruffled. Brendon stayed and had pizza with us. He's a doll."

"Oh, Sky's a big teddy bear. He just takes a while to warm up. He tries to put on that tough guy act, but that's all it is; an act."

"I suppose he has lightened up a bit."

"Are you two dating?"

Melanie's eyes grew wide. "What? No. We're neighbors. I wouldn't even call us friends really. Plus, he's dating some blonde girl."

Sam's mouth turned into a frown at that.

"Candace. He's not dating her; trust me."

Melanie got the feeling that Sam didn't care much for Candace. That was fine by her because she didn't either.

By the time they reached the bathroom, Melanie was overwhelmed by the third-degree questioning but managed to answer all of Sam's questions. She had a feeling that it was only the beginning.

Melanie took her time changing in the bathroom. She was none too eager to go back into the rapid-fire questioning. Skylar had said that his sister was forward. He wasn't lying. She slipped off her clothing exposing her high-waisted two-piece bathing suit. The top was a hot pink top that crisscrossed in the back and the bottom was a simple black. She'd worn bathing suits like it many times but, for some reason, she was nervous. She slipped on her bathing suit cover-up and slid her sandals on her feet.

When she emerged from the bathroom, Sam was standing in the kitchen talking to her mother wearing a strawberry colored bikini. She looked over at Melanie as she stepped out and smiled at her.

"Ready to have some fun?"

"Yep, lead the way."

The pair made their way out to the patio. More guests had arrived and were mingling around the pool. Melanie sat her things on one of the lounge chairs that were near the pool. Brendon and Sam came over and were discussing some games to play. There was a net set up for volleyball and a little basket on the side of the pool for basketball.

They decided on volleyball to start. Brendon went off to recruit some people to play with them. She looked around the patio for Skylar. Her eyes fell on someone she wasn't expecting to see; blonde bombshell, aka Candace. She walked in with a tiny dress that covered up her bathing suit.

What the hell was she doing here?

Sam leaned over and whispered in Melanie's ear. "I was hoping she wouldn't turn up since Sky canned her. She's relentless and can't believe that someone would dump her. She thinks she's the cat's meow. Really, she's just a stuck-up brat. Sadly, her parents know our parents so she's invited by default."

Melanie had no idea why Sam was divulging this information to her, but she was glad. She liked having some inside scoop on Candace, and she felt like she had an ally. They both watched Candace take off the tiny dress to reveal an even tinier bikini. Not much was left to the imagination. When she had her cover-up off she sauntered over to where Skylar was talking to his dad and Brendon. She stepped in the middle of the group and grabbed onto Skylar's bicep.

"Barf," Melanie heard Sam say under her breath.

She couldn't help the snicker that escaped her.

Candace looked up at Skylar through her lashes and shimmied her body closer to him. He wasn't touching her, but it looked like she was doing her best to climb into his arms. When he didn't respond to her advances, she hooked her arms around his neck and pulled his head down to her mouth. She whispered something in his ear. He reached up and peeled her hands from around his neck and turned to Brendon.

Brendon turned toward Melanie and Sam and pointed. Skylar nodded his head in agreement and the pair walked toward them. Melanie began to feel self-conscious. She knew she was being silly. There was nothing between her and Skylar. They weren't a couple. They weren't even really friends. They were neighbors that bumped into each other sometimes. There wasn't anything romantic between them, so what he thought of her didn't matter. He could have Candace.

The two men reached them and Brendon announced that they were about to get the games going.

"Better take off that cover-up, sweet thing, so we can get in the pool," Brendon winked at her.

"You are so full of it. You know that?" she retorted with a smile.

Grabbing the hem of her cover-up she hoisted it over her head. A whistle come from Brendon. She gave him a stern look.

"Shut it."

Brendon raised his hands in surrender. She looked over at Skylar who was frowning. Maybe he was shaken by his ex's presence, or maybe he didn't like the way she looked in her swimsuit.

She leaned over to him and asked, "You ok?"

"Yeah, why wouldn't I be?" He was still frowning.

"You're frowning, for one. For two, your ex is here, so I thought that was making you uncomfortable."

"She's not my ex, and I'm fine."

"Ok, if you say so."

She didn't believe his answer, but if he wanted to be moody then so be it. His attitude wasn't going to put a damper on her good time.

They got into the pool and began to divvy up teams.

"I get Melanie on my team," Brendon called.

Melanie and Brendon high-fived. Skylar, Sam, and her fiancé, Landon, all ended up on the other team. Brendon smack talked the other team boasting that they didn't need an even number to whoop them. He ensured that the other team was going down and that team B & M would dominate. They were about to start the game when Candace strutted over to the side of the pool where their game was set up.

Looking straight at Skylar, and in an overly sweet voice, she asked, "Do you guys mind if join? I see you're down a player."

CHAPTER ELEVEN

No one said anything. Skylar ignored her altogether. Sam broke the silence.

"I've never seen you play a sport. Come to think of it, I've never even seen you get in the water at one of these parties."

Candace pasted on a smile that looked closer to a grimace.

"I get in the pool...sometimes."

Brendon being Brendon spoke up. "I guess you can join in. We were going to dominate with just the two of us, but you can join if you want."

Even though he invited her, his voice was filled with reluctance. He didn't seem to want her to interfere with their dynamic duo, but he didn't want to be a total jerk either. Skylar gave Brendon a look, but Brendon just shrugged his shoulders.

"Great," she clapped her hands together and smiled while looking over at Landon. "I only have one request. Would you mind switching teams? I would love to be on Skylar's team if I can," she smiled brightly at Landon as she spoke.

Landon looked at Sam for guidance. She rolled her eyes and shrugged her shoulders. Landon nodded his agreement and swam under the net to join Melanie and Brendon. Candace sat down on the side of the pool and wiggled her fingers at Skylar.

"Skylar, babe, can you come and help me in?"

Skylar let his head fall back and looked up at the sky letting out a huff of breath. Annoyance radiated from him, but Candace didn't let that deter her. She was persistent. Melanie would give her that. He walked over to the edge of the pool and put his hand out to her. Candace pulled him close and placed her hands on his shoulders. Her body slid down his and she wrapped her legs around him under the water. Skylar kept his hands by his side in an effort not to encourage her.

Sam loudly cleared her throat, "Can we get this show on the road already?"

Candace gave her a sharp look over Skylar's shoulder but detached herself from him. Brendon and Melanie were both competitive to the point of being obnoxious, and gloated every time they scored a point. They were the perfect teammates. Melanie and Brendon won the first two games. Candace was not much help. She screeched every time that the ball went in her general direction. Melanie wasn't sure if she was afraid of breaking a nail or getting hit in the head. A good knock on the head may do her some good.

By the time their team took their third win, Melanie and Brendon had made up their own handshake. Skylar shook his head and laughed at their antics. He knew Brendon was crazy when it came to games, but he was surprised by Melanie's intensity. It made him like her even more. Not that he 'liked her' liked her although he couldn't deny that the bathing suit she had on accentuated every curve of her body. He never thought of himself as someone that was drawn to women with voluptuous bodies, but Melanie's was making him think otherwise.

"Dinner's done, kids," Arabella said from the side of the pool.

They all piled out of the pool and made their way to the long table overflowing with food. Skylar handed Melanie a plate and gestured for her to go before him. As she made her plate, he was right behind her making his. When she finished, she waited for him and they made their way over to a table to sit down.

Brendon, Sam, and their parents were already sitting at the table. Another man and woman that looked to be about the age of the elder Stillmans occupied two seats. Skylar pulled a seat out next to Sam for her. He leaned down to her ear and asked what she wanted to drink. When he ventured off to get their drinks, his mother looked at her with a warm smile.

"Melanie, we are so happy to have you today. Are you enjoying yourself?"

"I'm having a wonderful time. Your home is beautiful. Thank you for having me."

"It's our pleasure, dear. You're welcome anytime."

Skylar returned with their drinks just as Candace joined the table. She moved to the older man that Melanie didn't know and hugged him around his shoulders.

"Hey, Daddy," she said and kissed him on the cheek.

"Hey, princess."

Melanie tried not to make a gagging noise. Just her luck; she was sitting with the enemy and her parents. Figured he would call her princess. She sure acted like one.

Candace moved to the woman that Melanie figured was her mother and hugged her. Skylar, being a gentleman, held her chair out for her since he was still standing.

"Oh, it's so lovely to see you two together again," Candace's mom said.

She made a side eye at Melanie, but no one else seemed to notice. Skylar kept his head down and dug into his plate not even acknowledging the comment.

The conversation flowed. The men talked about sports, while the women talked about the latest books they'd read and celebrity gossip. Melanie contributed to the conversation as she loved books. She found that she and Sam had the same love for romance. They had some of the same favorite authors and books. The pair decided to swap numbers so they could talk about any new books they read.

The conversation turned to Sam's upcoming nuptials. She was gushing with excitement while discussing colors schemes, the location, and the honeymoon. Her fiancé held her hand on the table and looked at her with pure admiration as she talked so animatedly about their wedding. Landon was a man of few words, but it was clear that he was happy to be marrying the woman beside him.

Seeing the two of them so in love made Melanie a little sad. She longed for the day that she found someone who looked at her the way Landon looked at Sam. At the rate things were going with online dating, that day would be immediately following the day that hell froze over.

"So, Skylar," Candace's mother addressed him with a stiff smile. "Are you going to be taking a date to your sister's wedding? I'm sure that Candace would be happy to accompany you. After all, you're both going to be going anyway."

Melanie couldn't believe the nerve of this woman. Yeah, she wasn't there in the capacity of Skylar's girlfriend, but this lady didn't know that. For all she knew they were passionately in love. Yeah, it was highly unlikely, but it could happen. Before Skylar could answer, Candace jumped in.

"I would love to go with you, Sky. I assumed we would end up together once we got there anyway." She put her hands around his bicep again and smiled over at him.

Melanie glanced over at Skylar's parents and saw that his mother's mouth was set in a straight line. She didn't look pleased with the exchange going on between Skylar and Candace. Maybe she was angry that Skylar hadn't asked Candace already. Since they were family friends, she might've expected him to take her. Melanie stuffed a bite of potato salad in her mouth as a distraction. But, before she got it down, Skylar's words made her almost choke.

"Actually," he said as he removed Candace's hands from his arm. "I'm taking Mel with me."

He turned to her with a smile plastered on his face. His eyes looked frantic as he stared into hers. She took a big gulp of water to clear her air passage after her near-death experience. A large hand squeezed her knee under the table in a plea for help.

When she looked up from her plate everyone was looking at her expectantly. Everyone but Arabella, that is. She was looking at her with a small smile on her face. Melanie could tell she was trying to keep from laughing.

"Oh, well, yes. Skylar asked me to accompany him to the wedding."

There, that was non-committal. He did ask her, two seconds ago, and her answer did not confirm or deny if she would, in fact, be going with him. Sam started bouncing in her seat and clapping her hands.

"I'm so excited that you are coming to my wedding. Please tell me you agreed to go with him! We will have so much fun!"

Melanie held back a groan. How could she say no to that excitement? For some strange reason, Sam wanted her at her wedding. Melanie was a firm believer that a bride should have whatever she wanted, within reason, on her wedding day. Being at Sam's wedding was totally within reason.

"I wouldn't miss it." The smile she gave Sam was genuine.

Sam squealed and slung her hands around her neck in a hug.

When Melanie looked over at Candace and her mother, she could see that both of them were angry. Candace's anger was more evident than her mother's, but she could still see the indignation in the woman's face. Little did they know that she was as shocked as them. She and Skylar had some talking to do on the way home.

CHAPTER TWELEVE

A few hours later, Melanie and Skylar made their way out to his car. His mother and father walked them to the front door. They both hugged Skylar telling him to call them when they made it home. Arabella pulled Melanie into a hug.

She whispered in Melanie's ear, "Be patient. My sweet boy will see soon enough."

She released her with a smile.

Melanie had no clue what his mother meant by that. Was the woman insane? What would her "sweet boy" see? She wasn't sure how 'sweet' said boy was either. He was a royal pain in her butt sometimes, but she had to admit that his presence had come in handy from time to time.

Skylar opened her door as usual and waited for her to slide into the seat. When they pulled out of the driveway, his parents stood on the porch and waved until they were out of sight. Melanie thought about what Skylar's mother had said and about the wedding invitation. Melanie contemplated bringing up what she'd said. He probably wouldn't understand it any better than she did. She'd bring up the wedding, but she decided to give herself time before she ripped into him.

The way she saw it, she could still back out of the wedding. It wasn't her family, and it wasn't like she had to see these people again. They were gracious to invite her into their home, but she had no real ties to them.

"My mom really likes you. Sam does too," Skylar said interrupting her thoughts.

"Your family is nice."

"I hope you had a good time."

"I did."

"Look, I'm really sorry about the wedding. Mrs. Millis kind of put me on the spot. I panicked. I broke ties with Candace, and I don't want her getting any ideas that we are going to be a couple."

"Well, you might lose that battle because she is not going down without a fight. I don't think she understands the word 'no'."

"Yeah, she tends to get what she wants."

"I can tell. I don't know what to tell you, but I don't think I can go to the wedding."

"Why not?" his voice rose.

"Oh, let's see. One, I may have to work. Two, I barely know you or your family. Three, I feel uncomfortable."

"But you told Sam you would be there. She will be so upset if you aren't."

"I'll send her a gift. Besides, she won't even notice. She'll be too love-drunk to care who is there."

"Love-drunk?"

"Yes, you can totally tell that she and Landon are head over heels for each other. Their love is so obvious when they are together. It's beautiful really."

"She is happy," he agreed. "So what about me? You'll leave me to fend for myself against the Millis women? You aren't that cruel, are you?"

"You brought this on yourself. My suggestion is to not make rash decisions in the future, or maybe even stand up for yourself."

Skylar sighed. Even though it was dark, she could see the hard set of his jaw. She did feel a little bad for ditching him. His family was nice, and Sam was so sweet. It just felt like she was being played, and she didn't like that.

They were silent the rest of the way home. When they pulled up to their apartment building, Melanie got out of the car before he was able to get around to open her door. In the elevator, Melanie hit the buttons to their respective floors.

"Want to watch a movie?" Skylar asked looking up from his phone.

She stared up at him. Why was he trying to spend more time with her after they'd spent all day together?

"We just spent the whole day together. Don't you want to go relax alone or something?"

"No, it's still pretty early, and I don't want to sit alone in my apartment."

"Why don't you call up one of your friends, or go out or something?"

"You are my friend, and I'm asking you." He gave her a look like her question was idiotic.

"I really don't understand you, you know? I get to pick the movie."

"Fine; I'm going to change, and I'll be up in a minute."

Before she could respond, the door opened to his floor and he stepped out. She rode up to her apartment and made sure that everything was clean. After a quick browse through her movies, she settled on one. A few minutes later, there was a knock at her door. She opened it without looking through the peephole knowing exactly who it was.

Opening the door, she took him in. He'd thrown on a pair of sweatpants and a t-shirt that had been cut into a muscle shirt. His hair was damp from a quick shower. He cleared his throat and shook her out of her trance.

She opened the door wide enough for him to walk past her. She shut and locked the door and followed after him.

"So what's on tonight's playlist?" he asked.

"She's All That."

Skylar groaned.

"Have you even seen the movie?"

"Nope, I don't make a habit of watching chick flicks."

"Haven't you ever watched one with your mom, or Sam, or even a girlfriend?"

"I don't usually watch movies with Mom. Sam watches comedies when we're together. She saves the sappy bullshit for Landon. I don't do the girlfriend thing."

"You are a regular ol' Rico Suave aren't you, Mr. Stillman? This movie has comedy in it. You'll love it."

"Doubtful," he replied.

"Cry me a river. I'm going to shower real quick, and then we can start. You know where the drinks and snacks are."

Melanie headed to her bedroom. In the shower, she washed off the grime from the day. She twisted her hair up and wrapped it in a scarf then threw on a pair of PJ shorts with a matching t-shirt before heading back to the living room.

Skylar was sitting on one end of the couch scrolling through his phone with some sports show on the T.V. playing in the background. A glass of sparkling grape juice sat on the table next to a beer. Melanie picked up the glass with the bubbly drink.

"Thank you," she said.

"No problem."

Pressing play on the remote, the movie started. Melanie wrapped herself in the throw blanket from the back of her couch. A little way through the movie, Skylar moved toward the middle of the couch and claimed some of the covers for himself. Melanie felt her eyes getting heavy, but she couldn't fight them from closing.

She stirred from her place on the couch. When she opened her eyes the T.V. was back on the menu screen for the DVD. Something heavy rested on her leg. When she looked down, she saw Skylar's head and part of his torso laid over her legs. His legs were still hanging off the couch like he was sitting up.

Melanie shook his shoulder gently to wake him. He moved but didn't wake up. With a little more force, she shook him again. His eyes popped open and he looked around. He rubbed his eyes and finally seemed to remember where he was.

"Hi," he said looking up at her. His head still rested on her legs.

"Hey, you fell asleep with me as your pillow."

"I see that." He lifted himself off of her. "I didn't even know I was that tired."

"It was a long day."

"Yeah, it was." He stretched his arms over his head and Melanie took in his body. He sure was something to look at.

"I better get going."

"Yeah."

He pushed off of the couch and collected the glasses they drank from. In the kitchen, he loaded them in the dishwasher. When he reappeared, he held his hands out to Melanie.

"Come on, you need to lock the door behind me when I leave."

She placed her hands in his and allowed him to help her up. On her feet, she was only inches away from his face. He looked down, studying her, and ran his hand down her cheek then abruptly turned and headed for the door.

"Thank you for coming today."

"No need to thank me. I'm the one that should thank you."

He smiled at her. "Mel?"

"Yes, Skylar?" she tried to sound impatient but didn't pull it off.

"Will you please at least think about the wedding? I know I shouldn't have put you on the spot, but I would really like for you to be my date. I think we would have fun together."

He looked so sweet and genuine when he asked her. She wanted to stick to her guns and say no, but she couldn't. Not when he was so adorable.

"Ok, I'll think about it, but don't get your hopes up, Sky."

He gave her another small smile.

"You called me Sky. I like it when you say it."

He leaned in and gave her a kiss on the cheek and told her goodnight.

With that, she knew that she'd be going to the wedding no matter if she wanted to or not. He was too charming for his own good, and she was too dumb for hers. The least she could do to make herself feel slightly better about it all would be to make him wait for her answer.

CHAPTER THIRTEEN

Mel stayed busy at work the next day. They didn't have many appointments, but they did have a lot of walk-ins. Jade and Melanie had made plans with Claudia to meet up for their weekly drinks. Instead of going out, they decided to meet at Melanie's apartment for takeout and wine.

Once their last customers were gone, Melanie and Jade did their closing duties and left together. Claudia was going to pick up the takeout so they headed straight to her place. When the three of them were all there, they crowded around her coffee table and turned on some reality T.V. It was a guilty pleasure for all of them.

"So, guys," Claudia said around a bite of fried rice. "Work has been so crazy lately. There's been talk about layoffs and everyone's on pins and needles."

"That's awful, Claud. Are the layoffs a sure thing? Will it affect you directly?" Jade asked.

"I'm not sure. There are several of us that do similar jobs, so I'm a little worried."

"You're great at what you do, and no one is a harder worker. I can't imagine they would get rid of someone like you," Melanie said.

"I hope you're right. I don't know what I will do if I lose my job. I won't be able to stay in my apartment. It will just mess everything up. I am going to start getting my resume out there just in case."

Jade and Melanie agreed that being proactive would be the smart thing to do.

"You know," Melanie spoke up. "You could always focus more on your photography and get it off of the ground."

"Yeah, I guess so. I don't know."

"Well, if you do get laid off, you always have a place to stay here. I'd be glad to help promote your photography business."

"Aw, thanks, Mel." Claudia gave her a small smile.

Melanie worried about Claudia. She was usually the upbeat one of their group. To see her down and stressed was not the norm. Melanie prayed that her job was not at stake, but she meant what she said. If Claudia needed her, she would be there. Claudia had been her backbone when she didn't have one. Claudia had helped Melanie become the confident woman she was, and she would do anything in her power to help her friend.

The conversation moved to the show they were watching. It was one of the Real Housewives franchises. They talked about how they would act if they were housewives. Being stuck up and spoiled was something they all agreed that they wouldn't be. Remembering their humble beginnings would be a must. Jade and Melanie both decided that they would have a stellar wardrobe though.

A knock at the door interrupted their conversation about which housewives they could be friends with and which ones they couldn't stand. They all looked up in confusion. Melanie headed to the door. When she checked the peephole, she wasn't surprised by who she saw.

"Who is it?" Claudia yelled from the living room.

Instead of answering, Melanie opened the door for Skylar.

"Hello, Skylar. What are you doing here?"

"Hello to you too. Just in the neighborhood and thought I'd stop by."

She looked at him with a blank stare. "You live in the neighborhood, Skylar."

"Technicality. Can I come in?"

"Sure, why not."

Skylar scooted past her smiling as he went. She heard him rustling around in her refrigerator before he emerged into the living room.

"Hey, ladies. How's it going?" He asked popping the tab on a can of coke.

Jade muttered a greeting, but Claudia was much less subtle.

"What are you doing here?" she asked echoing Melanie.

"Jeez you and Melanie sound like a broken record. Can't I stop by to see a friend?"

Claudia squinted at him.

"When did you become friends? I thought you guys didn't get along."

"We get along just fine. Mel spent Saturday with me and my family. She's going to my sister's wedding with me in a couple of weeks."

Melanie stared at him with her eyes bugged out. This man was so exasperating. She had never agreed to this wedding ordeal and she knew he was up to something by telling her friends. Claudia turned her head slowly to look at Melanie. Jade was sitting in the oversized accent chair trying to hide a small smile. Melanie tried to busy herself by cleaning up some of the mess they'd made.

"Melanie Alyse Nova, don't you try to avoid me. Why didn't you tell us about this past weekend and the wedding?" Claudia was using her best mother voice.

Melanie groaned. She knew that the rat fink was up to no good when he came over. She knew that Claudia would take his side and guilt her into going. Jade would be the sensible and compassionate one. Claudia was relentless, and she knew that they were about to battle. She turned around to face Claudia.

"Yes."

"Don't 'yes' me. You know what I'm about to say. Why the hell were you holding out on us? You spent the day with a guy's family and didn't think to tell your BFFs? To top it off, you're going to a wedding with said guy. Next thing I know, I'll be getting a phone call saying you eloped in Vegas."

Melanie looked at Claudia with a bored expression. When Claudia got on her soapbox, it was best to let her run out of steam before even trying to say your piece.

"Are you finished being dramatic?" Melanie asked when Claudia was quiet for a few seconds.

"I'm not being dramatic, oh Keeper of Secrets. We're supposed to be besties, and you failed to mention some very big pieces of your weekend."

"For one, his family had a barbecue with their friends. It wasn't like I received a VIP invite to some exclusive party. Second, I never officially agreed to go to a wedding with him. He's delusional."

"Why aren't you going to the wedding?"

"What do you mean why am I not going to the wedding? I don't know him that well, I have a job where I work weekends, and I don't want to."

The last one was kind of a lie, but she would keep that piece of information to herself.

Skylar was sitting on the couch helping himself to their leftover takeout. He had a smug look on his face. The little stinker knew what he was doing. Melanie wanted to strangle him, but she didn't have bail money.

"You spent time with his family, Mel. You've been on a blind date for crying out loud. I know you, and I know you are just making excuses."

Melanie rolled her eyes at Claudia. Crossing her arms over her chest, she looked at her best friend. Or, at this moment, maybe her former best friend because she wanted to kill her. Couldn't she be on her side for once? Claudia was always throwing her under the bus.

Claudia just stared back at Melanie with her eyebrows raised. This wasn't the first time they had a stare off, and it most certainly wouldn't be the last. That was *if* Melanie let Claudia live. Jade and Skylar just sat silently watching the exchange. Jade was used to the two of them.

"These are not excuses, Claudia. These are objections any sensible person would make."

Instead of addressing Melanie's concerns, Claudia turned her attention to Skylar.

"You need a date for your sister's wedding, right?"

"Right," he replied around a bite of food.

"And you want Melanie to be your date?"

"She already agreed. My whole family is expecting her. They loved her, by the way."

Melanie eyes turned to slits directed at him. She stormed over to where he was sitting and snatched the takeout container from his hands. There was no way she was going to let him eat all their food when he was there to stir up trouble. He could get his own dang General Tso's.

"You put me on the freaking spot! I didn't know what to say, so I agreed."

"A promise is a promise, Mel. My sister is expecting you. Would you want to let the bride down?"

She wanted to put him in a headlock. Lucky for him, she knew she wasn't prison material. Maybe she could hire a good lawyer. Yeah, that's what she'd do, because Skylar Stillman was a dead man.

She needed a drink to deal with all the madness. She stormed out of the living room and into the kitchen. She pulled her sparkling grape juice from the fridge drank it straight from the bottle.

Skylar sauntered in while she was taking her first swig.

"Drove you to drink, huh?" He walked over and stood in front of her. "Got the hard stuff, too, I see," he said with a laugh.

She finished her swig and wiped her mouth with the back of her hand. Her inner savage had come out because Skylar was incorrigible. Before she could take another drink, he snatched the bottle from her hand and started chugging the contents. Her mouth gaped at his barbaric behavior. What the hell did he think he was doing? There was one thing you did not do and that was to come between her and her bubbly. She put both hands on the bottle and snatched the bottle from his lips.

"What's wrong? Don't like sharing?"

"I. Hate. You."

"No, you don't."

"Oh, but I really, really do."

Melanie stomped back into the living room where Jade and Claudia were sitting too close talking in hushed voices. They both looked up when Melanie entered the room with Skylar not far behind.

"So," Claudia started. "Jade and I were talking, and you are definitely going to the wedding. Jade said she will cover your shifts for that weekend if you are scheduled. We can go shopping this weekend for something to wear."

"Sweet," Skylar said giving the two traitors high fives.

"You know what? Fine; I'll go to the wedding, but not for any of you. I'm going because Sam is a sweetheart."

"I don't know how sweet she is, but she will be happy to see you there. My mom will be too. She keeps asking me about you."

Melanie couldn't resist an eye roll. She didn't know why his mom was asking about her, but what she did know was that after this wedding she wouldn't be seeing any more of his family. What she really wanted to know was why did he want her to go so bad? She was sure that he had his pick of women and could find his own date. Whatever ; after this, she was done with his shenanigans.

CHAPTER FOURTEEN

The next week went by in a blur. Between working shifts at the boutique and working on her blog, Melanie had been going non-stop. Before she knew it, it was the Friday before Sam's wedding. She'd laid out her clothes for the wedding and twisted her hair prepping it for a cute twist out in the morning.

She curled up on the couch with her e-reader and a fresh glass of juice. Her phone buzzed. It was a new text message. She scooped her phone up from the coffee table and swiped her thumb against the screen to unlock it.

Skylar: Ready for the big day?
Melanie: I guess.
Skylar: Don't sound so excited.
Melanie: I'm over the moon with excitement.
Skylar: I sense sarcasm...
Melanie: Whatevs
Skylar: Are you twelve?
Melanie: Bye, Skylar
Skylar: Be ready by ten. See ya in the morning.

Melanie woke up at eight the next morning. She gave herself enough time to make breakfast and to do her makeup. As she flipped her omelet, she heard a knock at the door. The clock on her microwave read eight-thirty. Still in her bathrobe, she looked down trying to decide if she had time to change. Another knock sounded. Nope, no time to change.

Skylar was on the other side. He was wearing running shorts and a t-shirt he'd cut the sleeves off of. Sweat covered the shirt. She drank him in. His body was worth perusal. What the heck was he doing there so early though? His message said ten. Opening the door just a crack, she peeked her face out.

"It's not ten, Skylar."

"Good morning to you too, sunshine. I know what time it is."

"Then why are you here?"

"I wanted to see what color your dress was. I want to make sure my tie matches."

Melanie stared at him. The man was crazy. Why had he waited this long to find out the color of her dress? He could've texted her to ask.

"Seeing as it is the day of the wedding, does it matter? You waited until the last possible second."

"I have a lot of ties. I'm sure I have something that matches. Let me see it." He put his hand on the door and pushed it open.

"It smells good in here." He tilted his head back slightly and took an audible whiff of the air.

"Thanks. The dress is pink. Now you can go so I can finish getting ready."

Skylar ignored her and followed the smell of food to the kitchen. He sat down at a stool that lined her breakfast bar. He gave her puppy dog eyes. Melanie huffed out a loud breath. She walked over to the plate where her fresh made omelet laid and placed it in front of Skylar. He gave her a big smile.

"Aw, we really are friends."

"You are testing my patience, and it is not even nine a.m."

She got the contents out to make herself another omelet. While she whisked the eggs in a bowl, Skylar stuffed a huge bite in his mouth. A moan escaped his lips.

"This is fantastic."

"Thanks," was all she gave in return.

"So if anyone asks, you are my girlfriend. My parents wish we were dating and, technically, this is a date. So..."

Melanie slid the fresh omelet onto a plate for herself and took the stool next to him.

"Why should I lie? Isn't it enough that I'm going? We don't even know that much about each other."

"You know about my family and what I do for a living. My family already knows we're neighbors, and that we met in the building. We'll tell everyone that's how we got together. It isn't even a complete lie. I'd say the basics should be good enough."

Melanie just shook her head. There was no point in arguing with his logic. She wasn't the one with anything at stake, anyway. They finished up their breakfast, and Skylar headed to his apartment to get ready.

At ten, she met him down at his car. He was leaning against the passenger side door in a tailored suit with a pink tie and handkerchief. When he spotted her coming out of the building, she could see an odd look cross his face. It looked like confusion and, if she wasn't mistaken, a little appreciation. When she reached the car, he stayed there a moment still leaning against her door.

"Um, are you ok?"

He shook his head and blinked his eyes. "Yeah, fine. You look pretty, Melanie."

Melanie rarely got shy, but she found her gaze move to the ground. If her brown skin would have allowed, a red tint would surely have graced her cheeks.

"Thank you. You don't look half bad yourself."

Skylar pushed off of the car door and turned around to open it for her. Once she buckled up, he shut her door. As he backed out of the parking spot, Melanie fiddled with his radio. A few seconds later, the sounds of a boy band blared through his speakers. When he turned his head to glare at her, she was bobbing her head and mouthing the words.

"What are you doing?"

"What do you mean 'what am I doing'? We're in a car, Sky. There isn't much to do."

"I told you about messing with my radio."

She snapped her fingers and did what he assumed were dance moves in her seat.

"Hey, I'm doing you a favor by going to this wedding with you to keep the blonde bombshell at bay. I think the least you can do is let me pick the music."

"Blonde bombshell?"

"Yeah, the pretty blonde you were screwing and are afraid of."

"I'm not afraid of her. She doesn't take 'no' for an answer."

"I hope you don't think your little plan will work."

"Why won't it?"

"Because no one, especially Candace, will think you would date someone like me."

His head jerked in her direction before he remembered he needed to keep his eyes on the road.

"What do you mean 'someone like you'?"

"Come on, pretty boy, you know what I'm talking about. You're handsome, fit, and seem to have a good job. You're what some would call 'the total package'. I'm short, plus-sized, and black. Your polar opposite."

"I don't know what any of that has to do with me dating you."

"Have you ever dated a black girl?"

Skylar's neck turned scarlet. "Um, I've slept with a few."

"Gah, Skylar, you're a pig. That doesn't count! Have you dated a big girl?"

"No, I guess not. That doesn't mean I wouldn't."

"Riiiight." Mel crossed her arms over her chest.

"It doesn't! I don't discriminate when it comes to beautiful women."

"Mm hm."

Skylar thought about what Melanie said. He had dated and slept with his share of women in his day. He'd never thought about the race or size of the women he dated. Well, that wasn't completely true. He was typically attracted to tall women. He was tall himself, so it seemed to make sense. Other than that, he didn't discriminate. He had been with some women with a few curves, athletic builds, and 'normal' physiques. No, he hadn't dated a black woman before, but it wasn't because from lack of attraction to them..

Skylar pulled into his parents' driveway. He walked around and opened Melanie's door and led her up to the house. It felt like they had walked into a circus. There were people running around with decorations. Caterers were hustling around with trays, glasses, and utensils.

Skylar's mom swept into the room wearing a beautiful, midnight blue, floor-length dress. There were tiny crystals scattered across the top. It tapered in at the waist and flared into a slight A-line skirt.

"Oh, Melanie, you look absolutely beautiful!" Skylar's mother brought her in for a tight hug.

"Thank you, Mrs. Stillman. You look lovely yourself."

"Call me Arabella, sweetie. No need for formalities. There will be eligible bachelors here tonight. I hope my son here is smart enough to keep you close by so none of them grab you right from under him." She gave Melanie a conspiratorial wink.

"Geez, Mom, please." Despite the exasperation in his voice, he scooped her up into a hug.

"What? I'm just stating facts, Son."

When Skylar released his mother, she turned her attention back to Melanie.

"Come on, dear. I'll take you to where the girls are. We have mimosas."

Arabella headed down the hall toward the stairs, and Melanie fell in step behind her. At the bottom of the stairs, she looked over her shoulder and waggled her fingers at Skylar. He was on his own for now, but hopefully Candace wouldn't be there anytime soon.

Skylar headed to the back patio to search for his dad and Brendon. They were standing on the lawn watching a crew set up tables under a tent.

"Hey, Sky," his dad greeted him.

"Hey, Pops."

He slung an arm around Brendon's neck and gave it a brotherly squeeze. Brendon gave him a light punch on the arm.

"So, I heard you were bringing your foxy neighbor," Brendon said.

Skylar popped the bottle tab on the beer his father had handed him. He took a big swig of the fizzy drink and relished in the cold liquid sliding down his throat. He would need all the booze he could get if he had to fight off Candace all day and night. Skylar wasn't an idiot, and he knew having a date wouldn't stop her. Candace was used to getting what she wanted, and she'd set her eyes on him.

"I brought Melanie. Mom dragged her off to be with the other women."

"Your mom seems to like her," Skylar's father piped in.

"Yeah, so does Sam. That's why I begged her to come for the last few weeks. That and I needed a buffer for Candace."

"Son, Melanie's a beautiful lady. I'd bet she doesn't stay glued to your side all night."

"As long as she is with me during the important parts, I think I can handle the rest."

His dad looked at him with a little smile on his face. The older Stillman was a man of few words, but when he said something there was meaning in it. Skylar didn't know what that smile was about. He chalked it up to the old man giving away his only daughter later.

A few minutes before four o'clock, Skylar met up with Melanie for the first time since they got there. He wasn't sure why they'd even had to be there so early since he wasn't in the wedding, but his mother insisted. So he, his brother, and his dad had hung out eating, watching T.V. and smack talking about sports. At one point, they even went into the room with the groom and groomsmen. His mother told them it was important for them to bond so that the photographer could get photos of them all. All Skylar knew was that he couldn't wait for the reception. He could drink and everyone else would be too toasted to bother him.

Candace hadn't appeared yet, and for that he was thankful. She had to be there by now. The wedding was about to start, and he'd seen her parents mingling with other guests. When she struck, he'd have his buffer.

Skylar led Melanie to the front row reserved for their family.

"Wow, I feel so VIP getting to sit in the front row at your sister's wedding." Melanie's voice seemed a little different. It had a lighter tone to it. He wasn't sure why. Maybe it was the wedding? Women always went all gaga over that kind of stuff. Skylar wasn't a fan of weddings. He figured he may settle down one day, but he honestly couldn't see it. He had dated and slept with a lot of beautiful women, but he couldn't imagine dating any of them long term let alone marrying any of them.

"You'll be surprised. She looks so beautiful," Melanie tried to whisper but failed. She then let out a giggle. He didn't think he'd ever heard her giggle. Then it hit him.

"Mel, have you been drinking?"

She looked up at him with her brown eyes. They stood out today. Her eyes were beautiful, he noticed. It had to be the makeup she was wearing.

"You could say that. We did a little pre-gaming before the nuptials."

"Mel, are you drunk?"

Her mouth dropped open and her eyes rounded.

"Skylar, this is a wedding. I would not get toasted before a wedding. I'm just a little tipsy. I'll save the real drinking for the reception."

Oh, goodness. Skylar hoped she wasn't one of those girls who got sloppy drunk leaving him to take care of her. He wanted to enjoy the evening not babysit. Only time would tell. He realized that she was his responsibility either way. He coaxed her into coming, so he would weather the storm.

Just as the music for the wedding party's walk started, Skylar spotted Candace. She was looking in their direction with a pouty lip and her arms crossed over her chest. She didn't look like a guest that was excited to be attending a wedding.

When she made eye contact with Skylar, she smiled and waved. *Oh, brother*, he thought, *and so it begins*. He made a curt nod back in her direction. Her unique brand of crazy needed no encouragement.

The backyard looked like something out of a fairytale. Up front, there was an arch draped in sheer white fabric and white flowers covered the top. A few yards from the ceremony, there was a tent that the reception would be held in. Servers from the catering company were shuffling around getting things set up for the cocktail hour.

Soft music played and two by two the wedding party made their way down the aisle to line up on either side of the arch when they reached the front. The first song faded out and switched to Musiq Soulchild's '*So Beautiful*', and everyone stood up. Sam and their father came into view. This was the first time Skylar had seen his sister all day. She looked stunning. Her dress was both elegant and simple. It hugged her curves up top and flared out by her feet. Pearls lined the sweetheart neckline. Her hair framed her face in soft beach waves.

When they reached the arch, their father handed her over to Landon. Skylar could see how much Landon loved his little sister. He wondered if he would, or could, feel that way about anyone. He looked down at Melanie and saw she was crying. She looked up at him with a weak smile.

"It's so beautiful. I love *love*."

It surprised Skylar to see her crying. She didn't seem the type to get emotional. Apparently, even she had a soft spot for weddings. He slung his arm around her shoulder and gave it a squeeze.

CHAPTER FIFTEEN

When the ceremony was over, Skylar and the rest of his family took pictures with the bride and groom. That left Melanie alone to mingle. She wasn't pleased with being left alone, but she'd manage. A group of women she'd met earlier stood sipping wine and chatting. Melanie joined them while they waited.

She scanned the area looking for Candace. She didn't see her at first, but spotted her flirting with a couple of men. She brushed her breasts against one man's arm. The other ogled them like he wanted it to be him. Melanie wasn't sure that Candace was as stuck on Skylar as he thought. The way she acted, it didn't seem like she was concerned with his whereabouts.

Another glass of wine later, and several conversations about single life and the latest celebrity gossip, Skylar headed her way. *Finally*, she thought. The women in the group were nice, but she'd been bored out of her mind. Skylar was a few feet from her when Candace came out of nowhere tugging on his arm.

When he realized it was Candace, Melanie saw him stiffen. He gave Melanie a pleading look. She downed the rest of her drink and excused herself from the group. By the time she reached Skylar, Candace had latched onto him for dear life. Skylar reached for her to pull her to his side.

"Hey Mel, I came to find you so we could get seated for dinner."

Candace looked at Mel like she wanted her to disappear. Before Melanie had a chance to respond, Candace raised her hand and turned Skylar's face to her.

Oh no-the-hell she didn't.

No, she wasn't there as a love interest of Skylar's, but still. That was rude. She was his date and, for all Candace knew, they were getting it on every night.

"Sky," Candace said with her lips in a pout, "I was thinking we could sit together."

Oh, puh-lease. Did this pouty face and whiney voice actually work on people? God help the idiot who fell for her tactics. It took everything in Melanie to keep from rolling her eyes.

"Sorry, Candace. Melanie is my date. I'm going to be sitting with her and the rest of my family."

Melanie saw the innocent, pouty look drop from Candace's face for a split second before she plastered on a fake smile.

"Well, save me a dance then, handsome."

Skylar just grunted in response while Candace made her way toward the tent.

The dinner went by rather quickly. The wedding party and some of the family made a toast to the happy couple. They cut the cake, did the first dance, and then the rest of the guests started to let loose on the dance floor. There was an open bar, and Melanie partook in the spirits.

Melanie felt pretty good and decided she needed to hit the dance floor. She tugged on Skylar's arm trying to hoist him up.

"Come on, Sky, let's go shake a tail feather."

Skylar groaned, "Do I have to?"

"Yes, you have to. You brought me here. The least you can do is dance with me."

Reluctantly, he stood up and followed her out to the dance floor. A fast song played. She grabbed his hands and began to dance around. Skylar wasn't much of a dancer, but he couldn't help but smile as Melanie jumped around and shook her body to the beat. She was having a blast.

A slow song came on, and Melanie wrapped her arms around Skylar's neck. He instinctively dropped his hands to her waist and held her to his body. Her curves felt soft against him. She laid her head against his chest and he could smell vanilla and orange. He wasn't sure how he had never noticed before. He pulled her body a bit closer to his, enjoying the feel of her in his arms.

She looked up at him and smiled. It was a beautiful smile, he noticed. Her eyelashes were thick and long framing her big brown eyes. He stared at her full lips that were painted in a deep pink color. She was a beautiful woman, but she was his neighbor. This was pretend, he reminded himself.

A light tap on his arm had him looking over his shoulder. He immediately turned his head back toward Melanie and rolled his eyes. She gave him a small smile and released her arms from around his neck. Candace stepped beside Skylar and laid her hand on his arm.

"Come on, Sky, dance with an old friend."

"I'm in the middle of dancing with my date, Candace."

Candace looked over at Melanie and quickly dismissed her.

"I'm sure she won't mind if I steal you for one dance."

"It's ok, Skylar. I can sit this one out," Melanie said.

He looked down at her urging her to stay. She just shrugged her shoulders. She knew that Candace would never leave him alone if he didn't dance with her at least once. Melanie was headed to the bar when Brendon came up and swept her into his arms.

"Hey there, beautiful! How about we show these people how it's done?"

He took her right hand and twirled her out and swung her back in. Then he dipped her. Melanie started laughing at Brendon's antics. The pair continued their moves through several songs. Skylar had his eyes on his brother and Melanie the whole time. To think she didn't want to come, and now she was like the life of the party. Candace kept going on and on about how she couldn't wait for her own wedding day and how romance was in the air.

"I knew that you weren't actually on a date with her, but now I'm sure if it," Candace said.

"What do you mean? Of course she's my date."

"Yeah, but it isn't a real date. She isn't your type."

"Excuse me? What would you know about my type?"

"Well, for one, you like your women a little more in shape."

Skylar just stared down at the woman for a moment. The face he once saw as beautiful looked shrewd.

"Her shape looks fine to me."

Candace let out a laugh. "Don't play dumb, Sky. You know she's fat."

Skylar stopped moving. Heat rose through his body. He dropped his hands from around Candace.

"Why did you stop?"

"I used to think you were gorgeous." Candace smiled up at him. "Then I realized that your outward appearance can't make up for your distasteful personality. Melanie is ten times the woman you are. She's beautiful, funny, and cares about other people. Unlike you, who only worries about what you can gain from people and situations."

Candace's mouth dropped open. Skylar surprised himself with his admissions about Melanie. He hadn't realized he thought those things about her, but they were true. Melanie was different from any other women he had ever dated or slept with. He enjoyed that she didn't seem obsessed with what he or any other person thought of her. She was just her.

"How dare you say those things to me, Skylar Stillman? That cow is not better than me. You will regret choosing her over me. When you come running back, I won't be there."

Skylar had all he could take of Candace's crap.

In a low and steady voice, he gritted out, "If I ever hear you insulting Melanie again, you won't be happy about the outcome. Remember, I know things about you that I'm sure you wouldn't want Mommy and Daddy knowing. I won't be running back, so don't hold your breath. Been there, done that."

Candace let out a screech and stomped off. Skylar hoped she left the reception entirely. As soon as Candace was out of sight, he scanned the room for Melanie. She was dancing with some guy he recognized from Landon's family. Her head tipped back in laughter as he spun her around the dance floor.

Skylar felt a pang in his stomach. It seemed irrational, but he didn't like seeing her dancing with the guy. He especially didn't like that she laughed so easily with him. If anyone made her laugh, it should be him; her date. He headed toward her and the guy. Melanie spotted him before he reached them.

"Skyyylaar!" she said in a very loud voice while still dancing. He knew she'd had a few more drinks since the reception started.

"Hey, Mel. Having fun?"

"Heck yeah, Jared and I are tearing up the dance floor, aren't we?" She looked up at the Jared guy and smiled.

He smiled back at her and nodded his head yes, not even acknowledging Skylar's presence. That annoyed Skylar even further. *Who did this guy think he was anyway?*

"Hey man, do you mind if I have my date back?"

This made the guy look up at Skylar. He then looked back at Melanie and asked, "This your date?"

"Yep, he's my date. Well, my fake date. He's actually my neighbor. I'm doing him a favor."

Why did she have to tell the guy he was her fake date? It was none of his business. The Jared guy chuckled at Melanie's confession.

"You aren't my fake date, Mel, and I would appreciate a dance with my date."

"Okay, okay don't get your panties in a bundle." She turned to Jared and gave him a quick hug. "Thanks for the dance."

"No problem, I'll be sure to text you."

She gave this joker her number?

A second later, a slow song came on. Melanie laced her arms around Skylar's neck like before. He wrapped his arms around her pulling her body close to his. A calm came over him that hadn't been there five minutes ago. He closed his eyes and enjoyed the feel of her body in his arms. He was exactly where he needed to be.

CHAPTER SIXTEEN

"So, who's this Jared guy?" He looked down at her to gauge her reaction.

"He's one of Landon's cousins or something. He gave me his number. We're going to meet up and have dinner or coffee maybe."

The look on her face didn't give anything away about how she felt about the Jared guy. Her voice was pretty neutral as well.

"Did you like him?"

"What's with the third degree, Skylar?"

"Nothing, I'm just asking. We're friends. Friends talk about relationship stuff."

She eyed him skeptically.

"I don't know if I like him. We just met. He seems like a nice guy and he showed interest in getting to know me better, so I figured why not?"

Skylar could think of a few reasons why not, but she'd had a few too many drinks for him to even go there with her tonight. He didn't understand his objections himself, but he knew they were there.

Skylar looked down at Melanie whose eyes were closed. It looked like she'd fallen asleep while dancing. He rubbed his hand up and down her back and whispered her name. Her eyes fluttered open and she looked at him. She was about two seconds from sleep.

"Do you want to go to bed?"

"I want to keep dancing, but I'm so tired," she mumbled.

A yawn escaped her mouth, and she buried her head into his chest. Skylar had to admit that he liked seeing this side of her. She wasn't as prickly. Sober and awake, Melanie wouldn't be so cuddly with him.

"Come on, Mel, let's get you to bed. We are having brunch with my family tomorrow so you can see some of these people again in the morning."

"Ok," she relented.

Skylar hadn't planned on staying the night at his parents, but it was late. He didn't feel like driving home. He had a few to drink himself and thought it better to be safe than sorry. Melanie followed him to his childhood room. It was how he had left it before college. Posters of his favorite sports teams and swimsuit models plastered the walls. He wished he'd taken down the half-naked women, but it was too late.

"Hey, I don't have any PJs to wear. You didn't tell me we were staying here overnight."

"It wasn't in the original plan, but you are asleep on your feet. I don't much feel like driving. I'd have to come back in the morning, anyway."

Skylar rummaged around in his dresser looking for an old t-shirt and shorts for them both to wear.

"Here," he handed Melanie a t-shirt with his high school's name printed on the front and a pair of basketball shorts, "bathroom's right through that door."

Melanie went into the bathroom. He heard the toilet flush and water running. A few minutes later, she came back out wearing the clothes he'd given her. She deposited her clothes on the desk chair. Skylar could see that she'd taken off her bra. He wanted to avert his gaze, but he couldn't seem to tear his eyes away. Lucky for him, she was tired and oblivious.

"You can go ahead and get in the bed. I'm going to go change too."

Melanie just nodded and walked over to the bed. Skylar used the bathroom and quickly changed into his shorts. He usually slept in just his boxer briefs, so he compromised. He wore the shorts but forwent a shirt.

When he walked back into the bedroom, Melanie was already snuggled under the covers. He slid in behind her. Melanie turned to face him.

"What are you doing?"

"Going to sleep; the same thing you're doing."

"We can't both sleep in the bed. Can't you sleep on the floor? Isn't there another room you can sleep in?"

"All the other rooms are taken by my siblings and family. No, I can't sleep on the floor when there is a perfectly good bed right here. It's a queen size bed. There's plenty of room for both of us."

Melanie didn't look satisfied with that answer. He thought she would argue, but instead she took two of the pillows and placed them in the middle of the bed.

"You stay on your side."

"Yes, ma'am."

* * *

Melanie felt the sun shining on her face. She didn't want to open her eyes. The bed was comfy, and she was still tired. Her body felt heavy. She assumed it was from all the drinks she had the day before. Her head hurt, and she wouldn't be surprised if she ended up nursing a hangover for the better part of the day.

Pulling her eyes open, she drew in a huge gasp of breath when her eyes focused on what was in front of her. Skylar's face lay inches from hers. Her head rested on his shoulder, and his other arm was draped around her and cupping her butt. No wonder her body felt heavy.

Before she could move his arm and shake him awake, there was a knock on the door. Melanie began to panic. She didn't want anyone, especially his parents, coming in and getting the wrong idea. Another knock sounded at the door.

"Skylar, are you in there?"

It was Sam. Shouldn't she be on her honeymoon or something? Why the heck was she knocking on Skylar's door at, well, she didn't know what time it was, but still. Skylar started to stir. When he opened his eyes, a smile crossed his face. She wanted to wipe the smile off of his face. He shouldn't be smiling when they were two seconds from someone walking in and getting the wrong idea.

"Morning," he said to her. He didn't move his arm from around her.

"That's all you have to say? Your sister is on the other side of the door, and we are in bed together."

"We aren't kids, Mel, and all we did was sleep." Not that he wouldn't have wanted to do more if she hadn't been drinking.

"Skylaarrr!"

"What, Sam? Good grief, why are you yelling?"

"Are you decent?"

"Yeah."

Melanie tried to pull away from him, but he wasn't letting go. She gave him a dirty look, but he just smiled in return. He was going to pay for this. He wouldn't know what hit him.

The door swung open, and Sam stood there in a white off the shoulder sundress and tan wedge sandals.

"Mom wanted me to wake you up so..." her words trailed off.

"So what?" Skylar prompted.

Melanie wanted to pull the covers over her head and hide. Instead, she waved at Sam.

"This isn't what you think it is, Sam. We just slept; nothing else. Your brother refused to sleep on the floor."

Sam looked between the two of them for a moment and then grinned. "I knew it," she said more to herself than to them. "Mom wanted to make sure you made it to brunch on time."

"What time is it?"

"It's ten-thirty right now, and brunch is at eleven."

"Ok, we'll get changed and be down there."

Sam gave them one last grin and headed out the door.

As soon as Sam was gone, Melanie pushed his arm off with force and sat up.

"Why didn't you tell her that nothing was going on?"

"Because it's none of her business, and you made it pretty clear. You sure know how to bruise a guy's ego."

"Yeah, but some backup would have been nice. I'm sure your ego will be fine. It's big enough to withstand quite a bit."

"It doesn't matter what I say. She's a romantic, so she will take whatever idea she has and run with it."

Melanie just crossed her arms over her chest and scowled at him.

"I don't have anything to wear for brunch, Skylar."

"Just shower and put on your dress from last night."

"Ugh, that's like doing the walk of shame right in front of your family."

"It's not the walk of shame if there was no sex and you took a shower."

Melanie rolled her eyes at his man logic. She didn't have much choice, so she showered, styled her hair, and put her clothes from the wedding back on. Once she was as ready as possible, they headed down to the dining area where his family was waiting.

CHAPTER SEVENTEEN

Everyone was seated at the table when Skylar and Melanie walked in. Melanie could feel her cheeks heating. Once again, her brown skin came to the rescue; hiding her embarrassment.

"Morning everyone," Skylar said in a sing-song voice as he pulled a chair out next to Sam and motioned for Melanie to sit.

She slid into the chair and mumbled her own greeting to the table. Skylar sat in the chair on her other side. He grabbed the plate of bacon and started to pile it onto his.

Glancing over at Melanie he said, "Go ahead, and dig in."

Melanie chanced a look around the table, and she saw Skylar's mom smiling at the two of them.

Crap, she thinks we did more than just sleep last night. She averted her eyes back to her plate. Skylar passed her the bacon, and she placed a few pieces on her plate.

"Melanie, how was your stay? I hope you were comfortable. I apologize that my son was so rude and didn't have you bring anything with you. I swear I raised him better, but sometimes it's hard to tell."

His mother gave Skylar a disapproving look, but Melanie swore she saw a hint of a smile.

"Everything was great. Thank you so much for having me."

"They looked pretty comfortable to me," Sam said.

Melanie wished the floor would open up and swallow her. *Could this get any freaking worse?*

"We were very comfortable. I slept like a baby. I may need to sleep with Melanie more often," Skylar said and shoved a fork full of French toast in his mouth.

Melanie choked on the sip of water she'd taken. She started to cough to clear her throat. Skylar patted her back, which was no help, while Sam snickered beside her. She was able to catch her breath.

"It-it's not what you think. We didn't sleep together. I mean we slept in the same bed, but we didn't sleep together. I put a pillow in the middle of the bed. There was nothing but sleeping going on."

When she finished her explanation, Melanie glanced around the table again. Skylar's dad read his paper oblivious to his surroundings. His mom grinned like her son hadn't just implied he had sex in her house. Sam smiled at Skylar, and he smiled right back like they were sharing a secret. Was the whole family loony?

Somehow, Melanie got through the rest of brunch without any more embarrassment. The conversation turned to yesterday's wedding, and she was thankful. Sam was excited to leave on their honeymoon and talked non-stop about their plans.

When brunch wrapped up, Skylar and Melanie got ready to go home. Melanie was happy to get home so she could take a nice, long bath and change into her comfy clothes. They said their goodbyes to Skylar's dad, Brendon, and Landon. His mother and Sam followed them out to the car. Sam hugged Skylar and then turned to hug Melanie.

"I'm so happy you came. When I get back from my honeymoon, we have to get together! You can come with me to my monthly book club. It's an excuse to talk about our book crushes and drink wine," Sam said.

Before Melanie could answer, Skylar piped in, "Mel prefers sparkling grape juice."

Sam smiled ear to ear and looked back and forth between the two. "Duly noted, bro."

"I'd love to join you at your book club, Sam. Goodness knows I love a good book, babe."

Skylar rolled his eyes behind her.

Arabella pulled her son into a hug and spoke quietly so only he could hear. "I really like her. I'm glad that you finally realize that you do too. She's good for you. You treat her well, and don't go embarrassing her and scaring her away."

"How did you know?"

"I'm your mom. No matter what you think, I know you better than anyone."

Arabella released Skylar and walked over to hug Melanie.

"We loved having you. You make sure that son of mine brings you back soon, ok?"

"I enjoyed myself. I will see what I can do. He doesn't like to listen to anything I say."

"I think you have the power to make him listen more than you think."

With a final squeeze, Arabella released her.

Melanie shook her head. She knew that Skylar didn't comply with anything she said.

When Melanie and Skylar finally made it home, she told him she was going to go home and relax. They were riding the elevator to their floors when Skylar moved to her and wrapped her in a hug. She was a little surprised at first, but she hugged him back.

"Thank you for coming with me. I hope you had fun. I was happy to have you as my date."

"I did have fun. Your family is great. Plus, I got a potential date out of it."

Skylar frowned and Melanie wondered what was wrong. When the elevator reached his floor, he stepped out and gave her a quick wave before the doors closed. Skylar's mood had done a one-eighty. She was halfway surprised he didn't try to bombard his way to her apartment. She was thankful because she needed time to decompress.

After Melanie took her much-needed soak in the tub, she called Claudia and Jade to tell them how things went. Claudia wanted a play-by-play in person, so they were all sitting in Melanie's living room with Real Housewives of Atlanta playing in the background while they talked about the wedding.

"I met a guy. We exchanged numbers and are supposed to get together soon."

"Yes, it's about time you go out with a normal guy. If you play your cards right, he might put out on the first night."

Leave it to Claudia to always take it there. Melanie rolled her eyes.

"I'm not giving it up to him on the first night. If that were the case, I could've done that at the wedding."

"That would have been kind of rude, since you were there with Skylar," Jade said.

"Oh please, Skylar wouldn't have cared. I was just a guise. It wasn't a real date."

"If you would have spread-"

"Claudia!" Jade yelled.

Jade never yelled.

"What? I'm trying to help her."

"More like pimp me out."

There was a knock on the door. They all looked in the direction like they would be able to see who it was through the wood. Melanie didn't need to super powers to know who it was. She opened the door not bothering with the peephole.

"Hello, Skylar, to what do I owe this visit?"

Skylar was standing in her doorway with Brendon in tow. They both looked nice in button up shirts, jeans, and boat shoes.

"We came to take you out. We're going to a place with a live band and drinks."

"No can do. Claudia and Jade are here, and we're hanging out."

Skylar walked past her into the living room. Brendon gave her a little smile and followed after his brother. Melanie fell in step behind them knowing there was no point in arguing.

"Hey, beautiful ladies," Brendon said.

"What are you two doing here?" Claudia said.

This time Skylar spoke up. "We came to see if you ladies wanted to go out with us. We're going to a bar that has live music."

"Hellz yeah, we're down!"

Curse Claudia and her big mouth. Melanie looked over at Jade to see her reaction. She gave Melanie a knowing look and just shook her head as to say 'what are ya gonna do?'. They both knew they were headed out to some bar with the Stillman brothers.

Claudia and Jade rode together, but Skylar insisted Mel ride with him and Brendon because they would be going back to the same place. When they walked into the bar, a band was already playing on a small stage in the corner. It sounded like they were doing covers of the top hits from the 80s and 90s.

"Want to grab a drink and find a table?" Skylar asked in her ear.

She nodded, and he placed his hand on her lower back as he guided them to the bar.

"What'll ya have?" the bartender asked.

"Jack and coke for me and," Skylar looked at her for her order. "Sex on the beach," she supplied.

The bartender handed them their drinks, and they made their way through the crowd to find the others. They had already snagged a small, four-person table and were gathered around with drinks. The bar was full, so there was only one seat left at their table and no other available chairs for them to grab.

"We can share," Skylar offered.

"How are we going to share that tiny chair?"

Skylar sat on the chair and then motioned for Melanie to come closer. When she did, he grabbed her drink and sat it on the table. He placed his hands on her hips and pulled her down onto his lap.

"There, perfect."

Melanie struggled to try to get up from his lap.

"Skylar, let me up. I'm too heavy to sit on your lap."

"Quit acting crazy. You aren't too heavy to sit on my lap. You feel just fine to me; relax."

What must people be thinking seeing her on his lap? They weren't a couple, but she imagined it probably looked that way to someone that didn't know any better. Skylar picked up his drink and took a sip. He started talking to Brendon about something. Melanie looked at Jade and Claudia for help, but Jade gave her signature shrug and Claudia was making lewd gestures. No help at all.

The band was pretty good, and the girls decided to hit the dance floor. They danced to song after song. Between Skylar, Brendon, and random guys they always had a drink in one hand. Mel took her time nursing just a couple of drinks. She'd had plenty to drink at the wedding.

"We need to come out with them more often," Claudia yelled over the music.

Melanie didn't know how many songs passed before they retired from the dance floor. When they reached the table, the guys were standing up.

"You ladies ready to get out of here? I have to work in the morning," Skylar said.

The trio all agreed they were ready to go. Melanie hugged Jade and Claudia and then headed to Skylar's car. Back at their apartment complex, Brendon hopped into his car to go home. Melanie and Skylar made their way into their building. On the elevator, Skylar pushed the button to Melanie's floor.

"I'll make sure you get in safe."

Melanie bobbed her head in acknowledgment. She was too tired to do anything else.

At her door, she fished for her keys in her purse. As her door unlocked, Skylar caught her hand before she could open the door. He wrapped his arms around her waist and pulled her into his body. He only had one drink at the start of the night, but Melanie could smell the faint scent of whiskey on his breath. He was so close. He looked down at her for several moments not saying anything. He looked like he was trying to work something out in his head. She was about to ask when his lips pressed into hers.

Instinctively, her arms laced around his neck. His hands moved down her back to cup her butt. His tongue licked the seam of her lips before parting them. She let out a soft moan. Her brain couldn't fully process that she was kissing Skylar, but it felt good.

After several more seconds, Skylar broke the kiss. His breath was coming out heavier than before. He stood behind her and turned her toward her door. He then reached around her and pushed the door open.

Leaning down close to her ear he said, "You taste even better than I imagined. This isn't over but, for the sake of my self-control, it is for to

CHAPTER EIGHTEEN

Melanie woke up to a banging sound. Her eyes opened and immediately closed. The sun coming in through her window wreaked havoc on her sleepy eyes.

The dreadful pounding came again.

Who the heck would be pounding at her door at, she looked at the clock to see the time, seven am on a Monday?

She buried her head under one of her pillows and prayed they'd grow tired and go away. Less than a minute later, her cell phone rang.

Why was the universe against her?

When she didn't answer the first time, the person called back; just as the door knocking resumed.

She snatched her phone from the bedside table wanting to deal with whoever it was quick.

"Hello?" Her voice came out in a rasp.

"Morning, sleepy head. You must sleep like a log. Don't you hear me knocking at your door?"

Melanie pulled the phone from her ear to confirm what she already knew.

"Why are you at my door, Skylar?"

"Come let me in, and I'll tell you.'

"Go away. I'm going back to sleep."

"No can do."

She now knew him well enough to know that he would, in fact, not leave her front door until she opened it. She hung the phone up without even saying goodbye. She sat up and rubbed her eyes to clear the sleep when a memory from the previous night came flooding back.

Oh crap; Skylar had kissed her. She couldn't go and face him. What would she say? How would she act? She needed to talk to Claudia and Jade. It was too early to bother them. Although, this *was* an emergency of sorts. Skylar banged on her door again; impatient man that he was.

Melanie realized she had no time to talk to the girls. She went to her closet and pulled out a hoodie and put it on over her tank top. Next stop was the bathroom to check her face. Thankfully, she had managed to take her makeup off and wrap her hair before falling into bed the night before. She splashed some warm water on her face and took the bonnet off of her hair.

Act natural, Mel. You can do this. If he doesn't bring it up, you don't have to either. Maybe they could act like nothing ever happened. With Skylar, she figured the chances were slim, but she could dream.

"Quit your knocking. I'm coming, crazy!" she yelled as she headed to the door.

"What took you so long?" were his first words when she opened the door. She was tempted to slam the door back in his face but, in true Skylar fashion, he was already walking in.

"Um, let's see... You knock on my door at seven a.m. when I'm still asleep. That should be explanation enough."

"I need to be at the office by nine, so we needed to head out early."

"Head out where? I don't have anywhere to be until eleven today."

"I'm taking you to breakfast."

"Says who?"

"Says me; now go put some pants on, and let's go."

"Did it ever occur to you that maybe I don't want to go? Or that you should ask instead of assuming?"

"You don't seem to like to do anything I ask, so this seemed like the most viable option."

Melanie rolled her eyes and started walking toward her room. "I'm ordering everything on the menu," she said before she closed the door.

***

Twenty minutes later, they were sitting across from each other in a diner a few minutes from their apartment. Melanie was looking through the menu trying to decide what she wanted. When she glanced up, instead of looking at his menu like she expected, Skylar was looking at her.

"What?"

"Nothing. Just admiring you."

Melanie let out a loud laugh and then covered her mouth in embarrassment.

"What's so funny?"

Was this guy serious?

"I think you know."

"No, or I wouldn't be asking."

Before she was able to answer, the server came up to take their order. Despite her urge to order everything and make Skylar pay for disrupting her sleep, she settled on cream cheese-stuffed french toast. The server scribbled down their orders and headed off to put them in.

"Do you remember last night, Mel?"

Aw hell, she thought that she would be able to avoid this awkward conversation.

"Of course, we went out with your brother and my friends."

"Don't be obtuse. You know what I'm talking about." When Melanie didn't say anything he went on. "We kissed last night."

"You kissed me, you mean."

A smirk crept onto Skylar's face.

"If I recall correctly, I don't remember you pushing me away. In fact, I remember your arms going around my neck and your lips participating."

Melanie covered her face with her hands.

"I had a few drinks. It was a momentary lapse in judgment," her voice was muffled through her hands.

Skylar stretched his hands across the table removing hers from her face. He didn't let them go as he placed them on the table. He held them in his and circled his thumbs over her wrists. She felt the touch straight through her stomach and down to her lady parts.

"Mel, that kiss was no accident. There was chemistry. I felt it, and I think you did too."

"I will admit that you are a handsome man. I think that any woman would be willing to kiss you, and would probably enjoy it."

"You think I'm handsome?"

"Really? That's all you can say?"

"Hey, you aren't giving me much to work with here."

Melanie pulled her hands from his. She needed to be able to think straight, and she couldn't do that with him touching her like that.

"Mel, I want to kiss you more. I'm attracted to you. I want to try to see where things could go with us."

"Skylar, I swear if you are playing with me; just stop. I don't know what you're up to, but it isn't funny. I did you a favor by going to the wedding with you to get Candace off of your back. I'm not going to play your pretend girlfriend because you're scared of some woman."

Skylar ran his hands through his hair and looked out the window. Melanie could see he was frustrated with her, but so be it. He was frustrating her with his antics. Finally, he looked back at her and she was surprised to see the intensity in his gaze.

"I'm not messing with you, Mel. I really am attracted to you. Something this weekend made me realize what had been right in front of me the whole time. Seeing that guy all over you on the dance floor kinda confirmed it. I was jealous, and I don't get jealous."

"Exactly, you don't get jealous because you don't do commitment. You are a playboy. You like a different woman for every day of the week. I'm not like that, Skylar. I'm not just a convenient lay that you can call when you have an itch."

"Goodness, woman! I don't want to just screw you. Well, I do want to do that too, but I want to date you. I know I don't have the best track record, but something about you makes me want to try. You drive me absolutely insane sometimes, but I like you. Maybe the fact that you don't bend at my every request is part of that. I don't know. I just know you're different."

As Skylar finished his mini declaration, the server brought their food. Melanie started to cut her french toast into bite-size pieces to busy herself.

"Mel?"

She looked up but didn't say anything.

"Will you at least think about it?" For the first time, she heard vulnerability in his voice.

She took a bite of her french toast, chewed slowly and washed it down with orange juice.

"Okay, I'll think about it."

***

Melanie couldn't seem to focus during her shift at work. She usually gave her clients her undivided attention, but she couldn't seem to keep her thoughts off of Skylar. The whole thing seemed surreal. The man didn't even like her when they first met, and now he wanted to date her?

She couldn't deny that she was attracted to him. He was a beautiful man. When he kissed her, she felt a sensation that she hadn't ever experienced with past boyfriends. The question was: could she trust him? Sure he was sexy and he had begun to grow on her, but his past with women was not ideal.

Jade had come in for the early shift and was about to head out for the day. Melanie decided to ask Jade what she thought. Usually, she would get both of her best friends together; she needed to talk this through now so maybe her head would stop spinning.

"Hey, J, can I talk to you for a second before you go?"

"Sure, what's up?"

"So, you know how we went out last night with Skylar and Brendon? Well, Skylar kind of kissed me in front of my door."

"What!" Jade's mouth dropped open, and her eyes were as big as saucers.

"Shhh, there's more. This morning, he came knocking at my door saying he wanted to take me for breakfast. At breakfast, he dropped this bomb on me that he's attracted to me and wants to date me."

Jade's mouth went from surprised to smiling.

"What's the smile about? The man has probably never had a real girlfriend. He probably doesn't even know how to spell 'commitment'."

"Mel, I know this is not what you want to hear, but I believe him. I really think he is attracted to you. I could tell there was something there but, at first, I don't think even he realized it."

"I thought Claudia was the crazy one, but I'm starting to have my doubts about you, J."

"Mel, I'm a quiet person. I observe people and my surroundings. I think your constant bickering has a lot to do with sexual tension. Yeah, maybe he has been with a few women; people change. Most people don't live that lifestyle forever. Even playboys settle down when they find the right woman. I don't think you should write him off for what he did before he knew you. At the core of it, you know he's a nice guy. Look at how he helped you when your car was broken, and you barely knew the guy then."

Melanie didn't like it, but she had to admit that Jade did have a point. No matter how much of a jerk he seemed at times, Skylar had done some pretty nice things for her.

"I guess you may be right. I just don't want to get hurt."

"No one does, but you can never succeed if you don't at least put yourself out there. That goes for anything in life."

Dang her for being so wise.

A few hours later, Melanie was locking up the boutique for the night. She stopped to grab something for dinner despite the fact that her stomach was in knots. She was nervous since she knew that the night wouldn't end without seeing Skylar.

Pulling into her parking spot, she sat in her car for a few minutes. Should she go straight to her apartment and wait until he came to her, or should she go to him? Knowing that she wouldn't calm down until she spoke to him, she had her answer.

Inside, she punched the button to his floor. She stepped out of the elevator and walked to his door taking deep, soothing breaths. She made herself knock before she had a chance to think and chicken out. For a moment, she didn't hear anything and thought maybe he wasn't home. His car was outside, but he could have been with his brother.

Just when she was about to knock again, the door swung open. His hair was a mess like he had just been napping, and he was wearing basketball shorts with no shirt. Who answered the door like that? Although, she couldn't complain. The view was pretty nice.

"Hey," she said.

"Hey, yourself."

"I, um...well," she was stumbling over her words. *Maybe I should have prepared a little better,* she thought.

She took a moment and closed her eyes before starting over.

"Yes, I'd like to give us a try."

CHAPTER NINETEEN

Skylar's arms were around Melanie lifting her off of the ground. His lips captured hers in a passionate kiss. He traced his tongue along her full lips before he slid it between them. His tongue caressed hers, and a faint moan escaped her lips. She was lost in him. The first kiss was good, but this one was better. It was hot and filled with need and a promise of more.

Still holding her, Skylar slowly ended their kiss. He peered down into her eyes and smiled his cocky smile.

"I knew you'd see things my way."

Melanie slapped him playfully and laughed.

"Cocky much? I don't think your head can get any bigger."

He slowly released her from his hold, and she slid down his body. He pulled her firmly into him. His length felt hard against her. "Oh, you have no idea just how big it is yet."

"That's not what I meant, you perv. You have a lot to prove before we do anything involving that."

Skylar pulled back and put his hands over his heart. "I'm wounded."

"You'll survive, I'm sure."

Melanie was relieved. She was worried that things would be awkward after they decided to give things a try. Aside from the kissing, which she thoroughly enjoyed, everything seemed to be normal.

"What's going on in that pretty head of yours?"

"I was just thinking about how normal this feels. I wasn't sure how things would be after I agreed to this."

"Things don't have to change. We can still hang out, but now I can touch you and kiss you; it's even better." He wiggled his eyebrows in a ridiculous gesture. "I do want to take you on a proper date. How about this Friday?"

"I suppose I can let you wine and dine me on Friday. What did you have in mind?"

"It's a surprise."

"With you, I'm not sure if I should be excited or a little worried."

Skylar scoffed at that. "Excited, obviously. I'm going to sweep you right off of your feet."

"We shall see about that, Mr. Stillman."

* * *

Friday morning, Mel woke up with butterflies in her stomach. She knew it was due to her date that night. She and Skylar had hung out a few times since they'd made it official. He'd crashed her dinner a couple of nights per usual. After dinner, they'd curl up on her couch and watch T.V. which always turned into a make-out session. She was becoming addicted to his kisses. One perk to his past was that he'd certainly perfected how to use his lips. She wondered if he was as skilled in other areas.

She was working the opening shift and had just sat down to review her clients for the day when her phone buzzed.

Skylar: Morning, I can't wait to see you tonight. Be ready by 7:00.

Mel: Morning :). I can't wait either. Where are you taking me?

Skylar: I told you it's a surprise. Wear a dress. Preferably something that shows off your legs.

Mel: You've been checking out my legs?

Skylar: Among other things.

There was a peach emoji at the end of the text.

That man. Melanie chuckled.

Melanie's day dragged by, but wasn't that always the case when there was something to look forward to? Despite her excitement, she focused on each client and gave them her undivided attention.

When five o'clock rolled around, she made a speedy exit. She needed to get home and start her beauty routine. She had been on many dates before, but she wanted everything to be perfect for her first date with Skylar.

After showering and lotioning up, she moved on to makeup. A video call from Claudia flashed on her screen. She answered it and propped the phone against her vanity, so she could continue her makeup. Claudia and Jade's faces appeared squished together on the screen.

"OMG, are you excited?" Claudia squealed.

When she told Claudia and Jade about her and Skylar, they had reacted as expected. Claudia did a whole dance including twerking through her living room. Jade just gave her a hug and told her that she was happy they were giving it a try. Sometimes, Melanie had no idea how the three of them were friends. They were so different in some ways but, somehow, they worked.

"I'm excited, but I'm also nervous."

"Why are you nervous? You guys hang out together all the time," Jade said in her soothing tone.

"I know, but this is different. This is a real date like a real couple. He's been with his fair share of women. What if I don't measure up to the others?"

"Mel, snap out of it! If he wanted to be with someone else, he would be. You said yourself that he never actually has relationships. That alone proves you are different. No man spends the amount of time he spends with you without having feelings. The man was busting into your apartment every chance he got even before you decided to date."

"I guess you're right, Claud."

"You're darn right I'm right!"

As crazy as she was, Melanie was thankful for Claudia in times like this.

"Okay guys, thanks for the pep talk. I need to finish getting ready. Skylar has a tendency to pop in early, and I want to be ready."

They said their goodbyes with promises of full details the next day.

Melanie was sliding on a pair of earrings when the knock on the door came. She smoothed her dress down and took a deep, calming breath. It was show time. She opened the door and was met with one of the sexiest sights she had ever laid eyes on.

Skylar was standing in her doorway wearing a pair of dark wash jeans, a light blue button-up, and brown lace-up oxfords. A sports coat tied the look together. He looked sexy as hell.

"Like what you see? I know I sure do."

"That ego, I swear. For once, you are right though. I do like what I see," Melanie said in what she hoped was a flirtatious tone.

Skylar moved further into the doorway and pulled her into his arms. He bent his head so that his lips were only a few inches from hers. Melanie's breath quickened.

"You look beautiful," he whispered before pressing his lips to hers.

At this rate, Melanie thought she may have to do a panty change before they even left her house.

"Alright, slick, let's get out of here." For her sanity's sake, but she didn't say that.

Once they settled into the car, Melanie asked, "Now can you tell me where we're going?"

"You're an impatient one, aren't you? I guess I can tell you the first part. I'll keep part two secret a little longer. We're going to dinner at Lula's."

"I've never been there, but I've heard it's delicious. I thought you weren't supposed to go to an Italian restaurant on a first date?"

"Maybe not, but we aren't a typical couple. We've shared enough meals that I figure we are past caring about that kind of thing."

Melanie turned her face toward the window to hide the smile that crept up on her face. He had called them a couple. She knew he wanted to spend time together to see where things went, but she didn't know he thought of them as actually together-together. It made her happy.

At the restaurant, Skylar helped her out of the car and held her hand as they entered. Lula's was an upscale establishment. They had the whole 'white tablecloth and fancy place settings' thing going on. Skylar ordered a bottle of wine. It was the most delicious wine she'd ever tasted. She would even consider trading in her sparkling grape juice for it.

Dinner was wonderful. They shared each other's meals, and Skylar held her hand over the table. He was attentive. Melanie realized it was the best date she had been on, and it wasn't even over. Skylar paid their bill, and they left the restaurant for their next destination.

Skylar wouldn't give her any hints as to where they were going next. He was surprisingly good at keeping a secret. About fifteen minutes later, they were pulling into the parking lot of a small building. The pounding of Latin music poured from inside.

"Where are we? What are we doing?"

"We're going to dance. It felt fitting since your so-called dance moves are what caused us to meet. I thought you might like to do some Latin dancing."

They entered the small building. The lights were dim, and the air was warm from all the bodies packed into the little space. People crowded around the small bar nestled in the corner. Along one of the walls, sat a small stage where a live band was singing and playing.

Skylar slipped his arm around her waist and led her to the packed dance floor. There were couples that looked like professional dancers and others that were stumbling through just having fun. Once they found a place in the middle of the floor, his hands went on either side of her hips and he began to move to the music. Melanie was impressed. The man could move.

"I thought you didn't like to dance."

"I don't usually, but it doesn't mean I can't. I kinda had a change of heart after dancing with you at my sister's wedding."

They danced until Melanie's feet couldn't take anymore.

"That was so much fun," Melanie said when they were headed back home.

Their intertwined hands were rested on his thigh.

"I'm glad you enjoyed it. I have to admit; I did too. I wanted this to be the perfect first date."

"You definitely succeeded. This was the best date I've ever had."

Skylar lifted their hands and kissed the back of hers. "The first of many, I hope."

CHAPTER TWENTY

The next day, Melanie was sitting on her patio drinking her signature bubbly and reading. Her phone rang, and she was happy to see it was her dad. A pang of guilt hit; she hadn't called him first.

"Hey, Dad."

"Hey, sweetie. How are you?"

"I'm good. Just sitting out on my patio reading a book."

"You always have been a bookworm. How are work and your blog?"

"Work is good. Business has been up since it's a new season, so that's been great. The blog is going well. I need to find more time to devote to it, but it's getting there."

"That's great, sweetheart."

"How are Gwen and her garden?"

"Oh, Gwen is doing just fine. Her garden is blooming quite nice. You will have to see it when you come visit."

Ah, there it was. She knew she couldn't get away without any hint of her visiting soon.

"I'm sure I will, Dad. How are you holding up?"

"Not too bad for an old man. I'd be even better if I got to see my little girl."

"I'm not little anymore, Pops."

"You'll always be my little girl." They were silent, both reflecting on how much things had changed over the years.

"Anything else going on in your life that you want to talk about?"

Melanie didn't know how he did that, but her father always knew when there was something going on with her. When she was younger, she hated it. Now that she was older and her mom was gone, it was nice. Her father understanding her made all the difference.

"There is something. I'm kind of seeing someone. He's my neighbor. We started out as friends. Well, friends may be a stretch, but I was his date to his sister's wedding and things just escalated from there."

"That's great, honey. Does he treat you well?"

"Yeah, he does. We got off to a rocky start, but he's been really helpful since I met him. He helped me when I had car troubles even before he knew me very well."

"He sounds like a good young man. I sense some hesitation."

Melanie didn't know how much she should tell her dad. Claudia and Jade were great to talk to, but sometimes advice from an actual male point of view, especially one that knew her so well, was helpful.

"He doesn't have the best track record with relationships. I don't think he did relationships before this. Suddenly, he wants to try it out with me. I don't know if I trust that he has or even can change his ways."

"Mel, sometimes it just takes that one person to change the way we look at life. Maybe you are his person. You're a good judge of character. I think you'll be able to tell if anything's up."

"I hope you're right, Dad."

"Of course I am. My daughter is one smart cookie."

Melanie ended the call with her father and grabbed the notebook she jotted her blog ideas in. She made a tentative schedule of posts for the next few weeks. If she was going to grow her audience and gain clients for her side hustle, she'd have to be organized. With her schedule planned out, all she had left to do was to ask Claudia if she could take her photos.

Her phone buzzed again, but this time it was a text message.

Skylar: Brendon and Sam are over and we're having pizza. Come down. Already got your drink.

Melanie smiled at her phone. He'd gone from driving her crazy to being the highlight of her day. The fact that he did something as small as having her favorite drink was sweet. As sweet as he might be, she still liked to push his buttons a little. Instead of responding, she went into the bathroom to freshen up. She stood in front of her closet trying to decide if she should change. A comfy pair of leggings and a v-neck t-shirt were what she chose. She thought Skylar may appreciate her 'peach' in leggings.

Locking the door behind her, she headed to his apartment.

When she knocked on the door, it swung open and Brendon picked her up in a bear hug. She let out a squeal and laughed at Brendon's antics.

"Hey, ya big goof. Put me down, will ya?"

"It's not every day I get to see a pretty lady. How are you, beautiful?"

Strong arms wrapped around Melanie's waist. These arms were more than welcome.

"Back off, bro, I got dibs on her. Go find your own girl."

Melanie turned her head to look over her shoulder. "Aww, is little Skylar jealous?"

His arms tightened around her, and he planted a wet kiss on her cheek. "Dang right I am!"

Melanie laughed at the brothers. She wasn't accustomed to the outward affection that Skylar was showing. It would take some getting used to although she didn't doubt for a second that their bickering wasn't over for good. That was just how they were. Now she got a make-up and make-out session; that, she could live with.

Skylar buried his nose into Melanie's neck and inhaled.

"I thought you weren't coming since you didn't answer my text." His lips vibrated against her skin. Chills ran down her spine.

"I figured I'd keep you guessing."

"Is that so?" He pressed light kisses on her neck and behind her ear.

"Mmm hmm," she moaned in response.

"I'm getting some major third wheel vibes. I'll be in the living room when you two are finished groping each other."

Brendon made a show of scooting past them and shielding his eyes. He was such a drama king sometimes. Melanie loved it.

"Where's the pizza? I was promised cheesy goodness upon my arrival."

"It's in the living room. Go on ahead, and I'll bring your drink."

Skylar released Melanie from his hold, and she joined Brendon and Sam. She felt a smack then a squeeze on her behind. She stopped in her tracks turning to Skylar. He had a boyish smile on his face.

Shrugging his shoulders, he said, "I'd say I'm sorry, but I'm not. I couldn't help myself."

He winked at her and then passed by to go into the kitchen. When Melanie collected herself, she couldn't stop her own smile.

"There you are! I thought you were going to leave me alone with these two buffoons."

Sam got up from her seat and threw her arms around Melanie. Melanie returned the hug.

"I wouldn't subject you to that kind of torture, Sam."

Skylar came into the room with Melanie's drink. She grabbed a plate and a couple pieces of pizza before settling onto the couch. Skylar sat beside her and rested his arm behind her on the back of the couch. The four of them chatted about the show they were watching, work, and other random things.

"Guys, we should go out this weekend. We could all go bowling, or something fun," Brendon said.

"I can't. I'm going shopping and having a spa day with Mom and some of her friends. Mel, you should totally go with us. It will be fun!" Sam's voice rose an octave in her excitement.

"Oh, I wouldn't want to impose on your outing."

Sam had her phone out and was typing away.

"You won't be imposing. The more the merrier. Plus, I just sent Mom a text, and she says you have to come too!"

"Okay, if you're sure."

Sam squealed and clapped her hands together.

Before she left, Sam gave Melanie the details of the outing. She promised to text her leading up to it with any more information she may need.

When Sunday came, Melanie was nervous. She'd already spent time with Skylar's mother and Sam on several occasions, so she wasn't really worried about them. She was more worried about their social circle. Skylar's family seemed refined and elegant. Melanie wasn't sure if their friends would be as nice as them, or if they'd be stuck up like Candace and her family.

Melanie pulled up to the country club. Sam was waiting for her outside of the door as promised. It helped to know that she wouldn't have to walk in alone. Skylar had come over before she left and tried to give her a pep talk that turned into hot kisses and heavy petting.

"Ready to do this?" Sam asked when Melanie reached her.

"As ready as I'll ever be. I may need a mimosa to take the edge off."

"Girl, you are in luck because we have unlimited mimosas coming our way."

Sam linked her arm in Melanie's and led her into the dining area. The two were making their way through tables when Melanie spotted Mrs. Stillman talking to another woman that looked about her age. She scanned the rest of the table seeing if she recognized anyone from the wedding.

Her steps faltered before she came to a complete stop. This could not be freaking happening. Sam wouldn't have invited her knowing that she'd be there. Sam turned to Melanie with a furrowed brow.

"What is it, Mel? Is everything ok?"

"Why didn't you tell me?"

"Tell you what?"

Sam followed her gaze to their table. Melanie heard her mutter 'crap' under her breath.

Candace was sitting beside her mother in a white sundress. Her hair was straightened and laid perfectly on her shoulders. Her makeup was flawless. She was perfectly put together. Melanie tried to pull her arm from Sam's. She hoped that no one saw her so she could exit without anyone realizing.

Sam tightened her grip. She was pretty strong for being so small.

"Mel, I'm so sorry. I didn't know that they were invited. I didn't expect Candace to come. She never comes."

"It must be my lucky day then." Melanie's tone was dry.

"Come on, Mom knows you are coming. She will be disappointed if you leave. I promise I won't leave your side today. We will avoid her and act like she isn't even here."

Melanie was quiet for a second thinking about what she should do. Mrs. Stillman spotted them and waved. It appeared her mind had been made up for her. She huffed out a breath. Those unlimited mimosas would come in handy. It was going to be a long flipping day.

CHAPTER TWENTY-ONE

When Melanie and Sam approached the table, Arabella stood and hugged them both.

"I'm so happy you could join us, dear."

"Thank you, Mrs. Stillman."

"You know to call me Arabella. No need for formalities. Especially now that that son of mine got his head out of his behind." She winked at Melanie.

"Ladies, this is Melanie, Skylar's girlfriend. Some of you may have met her at the wedding."

Melanie waved at the table. They all gave her warm hellos in return. All except for two. Melanie looked at Candace and her mother out of the corner of her eye. Candace was scowling with her arms crossed over her chest. Her mother was leaned over whispering something in her ear. Melanie assumed it was something about her.

The best tactic would be to ignore them. She wouldn't speak to them. Hopefully, they wouldn't speak to her. Melanie and Sam got settled into their seats, and the server came to take their orders. Once they were gone, the conversations began to flow.

Melanie was talking to one of Arabella's friends named Cathy who was an editor for a local women's magazine. Melanie told her about her blog and the boutique she worked at. Cathy seemed very interested in checking out both her blog and the boutique. With any luck, maybe Melanie could design a few looks for a spread in their magazine.

"So, Melanie," Candace's mom interrupted her thoughts about the magazine spread. "How long have you and Skylar been together?"

So, they were going to go there.

"Oh, not too long. We've been neighbors for a couple of months now."

She kept it vague.

"Huh, funny he didn't mention you when he came to our house for dinner the last time."

Had he been at their house for dinner? Melanie chastised herself. Of course he had; they were family friends. She was sure that it had been before they were official. Skylar had been running from Candace from the moment she met him.

Melanie didn't respond. What was there to say? The woman was clearly trying to get under her skin. She wasn't going to let her. The rest of brunch was nice. The food was top notch, and the ladies were wonderful.

After breakfast, they got massages and facials. There was a hot tub they relaxed in while the other ladies were having their turn getting pampered. They finished the day with pedicures. Melanie and Sam had side-by-side chairs.

"What color are you getting?"

"Hm, I don't know. Probably light pink."

"Good call. I'm going with red. Scooch over here; let's take a selfie and send it to my brother."

"Um, do we have to?"

"Yes, come on. Guys like that kind of thing."

"Why don't you send a picture to Landon?"

"Already have."

"Fine, but just one. I can't have him thinking I like him too much. He has a big enough head already."

Melanie was smiling despite her words. She liked being in a relationship with Skylar. But it had been a while since she'd had a relationship and she was shy about some things. On top of that, Skylar was sexy as all get out. Melanie smiled for Sam's picture then sat back to relax. A minute later, her phone vibrated.

Skylar: I see Sam roped you into a selfie. She gets me all the time. I hope you're having fun with the ladies.

Mel: Yes, against my best judgment, I let her snap one. I guess it makes us official. Your friend Candace is here, so it's a bit awkward. I'm getting through it. Mimosas got my back.

Skylar: Crap, Mel, I didn't know she would be there. I'm really sorry. I see her presence made you go for the hard stuff. As for the picture, I'm cropping my sister out and saving you as my phone background.

Mel: For the love of God, don't set that picture as your background.

Skylar: Why not?

Mel: It's not a great picture, and there's no need.

Skylar: Too late.

The man knew how to push her buttons and make her swoon all at the same time. Melanie saw someone sitting in the chair on the opposite of her. She glanced up, and it was Candace. So much for a drama free day.

"Hi, Melanie."

"Candace."

"So, you and Skylar, huh?"

"Yep."

Where was this chick going with this?

"I have to admit, I didn't believe it when we were at the wedding. I figured he was playing hard to get."

Was she for real? Melanie balled her hand into a fist at her side where Candace couldn't see it.

"Nope."

"Good for you. I'm sure this whole thing is new for you. Skylar's a pretty sought after guy. It takes a certain type of woman to keep his attention."

Candace clearly thought she was the type to keep his attention. Too bad he ran the opposite direction when he saw her.

"Has he shown you the thing he does in bed yet? Gah, I love when he does that. Don't you?"

What thing was this heffer talking about, and why was she using present tense? She better be talking about a distant memory. No, Melanie and Skylar hadn't been physical yet, but she didn't think he would step out on her; especially with Candace. Melanie knew that he was used to sex, and a lot of it. He said he wanted to change. She had to trust that.

"Oh, got to go, Mom's waiting for me."

With a fake wave and smile, she walked away on her heel clad feet.

When Melanie pulled up to her building, she was happy to be home. She enjoyed the company of the women, but Candace had left a sour taste in her mouth. In the elevator, she considered stopping at Skylar's floor but decided against it. She needed time to process the events of the day.

At her door, her breath caught in her throat. There was a vase full of pink and white daisies. Beside the vase was a bottle of her sparkling juice. A card stuck out of the flowers.

'I've never done anything like this before but, when I saw these, I thought of you.

I hope this proves I'm taking my boyfriend status seriously.
-Sky'

Melanie's face broke into a grin. He was better at this than he let on. She let herself into the house and put the flowers on the living room table. She dialed Skylar's number. He picked up on the second ring.

"You got my gift." It wasn't a question.

"I did. They're beautiful, Skylar; thank you."

"So are you."

"Stop," she said in a not so convincing voice.

"I can't. I like complimenting my girl."

Before she answered, there was a knock at her door. She ended the call knowing that it was him.

As soon as the door was open, his arms were wrapped around her waist and his lips fused to hers. She moved her hands through his hair loving the silky feel of it against her fingers. He backed her further into the apartment until they were in front of the couch. He sat down and pulled her on top of him.

He cupped her backside pulling her closer into him. His hands slowly made their way up her hips and under her shirt. His strong hands caressed her back. She stiffened slightly; a little self-conscious of him feeling her lumps and rolls.

"I love the feel of your body."

Well dang. She tried to focus on his words and not let her insecurities win. Melanie's body reacted to Skylar's touch. It yearned for a long overdue release. The encounter with Candace had reminded her why she wanted to take it slow. She mustered up all of her willpower and pulled away. Skylar's eyes fluttered open.

"Why'd you stop?" His hands rested on her hips.

"I didn't want to get too carried away. It's not that I don't want to. I want to. It's just that I want to take it slow."

Skylar's head dropped forward, and he rubbed the back of his neck with his hand.

"This has to do with Candace, doesn't it? When you told me she was there, I knew nothing good could come from it."

"No. Well, kind of. She just said something that made me realize there's no need to rush. If we're truly into each other, things will lead to that. I want to trust you, Skylar, but I need time to get used to this."

Skylar pounded his fist against the back of the couch and cursed.

"I understand, and I respect your decision. I'm just angry that Candace can't let me live my life. She can't seem to imagine that not every guy is going to fall at her feet."

"She can't stand that someone like me has what she wants. It's probably killing her."

Skylar leaned in and pressed a light kiss on Melanie's lips.

"I like what I have just fine, and I don't plan on letting go."

He swatted her behind. She giggled. Melanie loved how he made her feel.

CHAPTER TWENTY-TWO

Melanie was sitting at her desk the next morning sipping on her first cup of coffee when she got a text message. It was the group thread with Claudia and Jade.

Claudia: 911! Drinks tonight right after you two get off work.

Oh crap, it had to be something major if she used '911'. Jade came rushing into Melanie's office just as she was about to reply.

"What do you think's going on?"

"I'm not really sure, but it must be something serious," Melanie replied.

"I hope she's ok. Should we try to get out of here early?"

"I'm going to text her now and see what she says."

Mel: Claud, is everything ok?

Claudia: No! I've been laid off.

Melanie looked at Jade who was reading the same text message.

"We need to get out of here as soon as we can."

Jade nodded her head. "Agreed."

The earliest Melanie and Jade could leave work was five. They went to the grocery store to get the essentials: pizza and chocolate. The trio met at Claudia's house, so she'd be in the comfort of her own home when she passed out.

Claudia opened her door with a glass already in hand. She'd had a head start on drowning her sorrows.

"Hey, ladies," her words were already beginning to slur.

Jade and Melanie looked at each other. Things may have been worse than they thought. Melanie wasn't sure why she was surprised since Claudia had all day to start. The girls made their way into the kitchen to cook the pizza and start snacking on the rest.

"I already have the wine open. Help yourself, ladies. I've been helping myself all day because I had nothing better to do."

Claudia burst into a fit of giggles. Her giggles turned into sobs. She plopped down on one of the stools lining her counter. She put her head on the table and shook it back and forth; the cries not letting up.

Melanie moved over to her best friend and put her arm around her shoulder.

"I can't believe it really happened. There'd been talk of it, but that still doesn't prepare you for it."

Melanie rubbed soothing circles on Claudia's back trying to comfort her.

"How am I going to pay rent and my bills?"

"Claud, you were outgrowing your position there anyway. You've been talking about finding something different or trying to grow your photography. I know it sucks, but this might be the push you needed. You know that you can stay with me if you need to, but I don't think it will come to that. We'll help you find something new. I'll ask around to see if anyone I know knows of any openings. It's going to work out."

"Yeah, Mel's right. It's the perfect time for you to focus on your photography," Jade added.

"If you want to take pictures for my blog, I'll be glad to give you a shout out and put links to your portfolio. We can make this happen," Melanie said.

Claudia wiped her eyes with a napkin. She heaved in a few deep breaths.

"You guys are right. I have wanted to focus on my photography. Worst case scenario, I'll go stay with my parents for a while."

"You have us and your parents. We're in your corner."

She sniffled a few more times before nodding her head in agreement.

The trio feasted on pizza and snacks while talking about their goals, dreams, and life in general. They started planning ideas to get Claudia's name out there as a reputable photographer. She was truly talented and, with the right marketing and word of mouth, her business could grow in no time. The night started as a crisis, but turned into an introspective girls' night.

"Mel, how is your sexy neighbor? Or should I say *boyfriend* now?" Claudia wasn't too drunk to talk about Melanie's love life.

"He's good. We're good. It's still weird to call him my boyfriend. I think of us as dating."

"What's the difference?" Jade asked.

"Nothing, I suppose. Dating just sounds less official; not so serious."

"Girl, you better call that man your boyfriend. I don't know what kind of BS thoughts you have in that crazy head of yours, but he only has eyes for you these days." Even under the influence, Claudia was blunt and insightful.

"Whatever the case may be, we're taking it slow. I don't want to jump into anything too fast."

Claudia looked over at Melanie. "That's your way of saying you aren't giving up the P. If you don't let that man devour your body, you are insane."

"It's clear that alcohol doesn't give you any more discretion than normal," Melanie rolled her eyes at Claudia. It was in vain because Claudia was back to chugging wine. "I just need more time to be sure that he is going to be serious about us and will be faithful. I don't need any more jerks. I'm tired of dating all the wrong guys."

"I see the way he is with you, and I say he's all in. Don't cut yourself off from something that could be great," Claudia said.

Melanie couldn't stop the silly grin that crept onto her lips.

"Fine, he's my boyfriend. Gaaaahh, I would have never guessed that he and I would be a thing, but somehow it happened. I can't say that I'm mad about it either. Even though he knows how to push my buttons, he can also be sweet. Not to mention he is pretty sexy."

"That a girl!" Claudia was definitely three sheets to the wind. Her words were loud and running together.

Jade and Melanie waited for Claudia to pass out. It didn't take long. They cleaned up the kitchen and left a bottle of water and some aspirin beside her bed. She'd need it in the morning.

When Melanie got home, the first thing she thought of was Skylar. She hadn't seen him all day. She'd gotten pretty used to seeing him on a regular basis with his impromptu visits. In a split decision, she hit the button for his floor. He wasn't the only one that could drop by unannounced.

Melanie smiled as the doors opened to his floor. The familiar feeling of butterflies flying around in her stomach was undeniable. She reminded herself that this was just Skylar, her pesky neighbor. It calmed her nerves to think of him like that opposed to thinking of him as her smoking hot boyfriend that she wanted to tear her clothes off for and let him have his way with.

Her nerves calmed down and she knocked on his door. At first, she didn't hear anything. She should have texted him first. So much for spontaneity. Just as she was about to turn back to the elevator, there were footsteps and the door opened.

Relief flooded her. The door opened a crack and Melanie's heart dropped. Candace's face was staring back at her. She was wearing one of Skylar's shirts and no pants.

So many thoughts were invading Melanie's mind, starting with *'What the hell?'*

"Oh, Melanie. Funny to see you here."

Huh, funny to see her there? Was this chick joking?

"I could say the same for you."

Candace let out a laugh that sounded remnant of a hyena.

"Skylar and I just got done having a little fun. I knew he wouldn't be able to stay away long. He's in the shower now. Did you need him for something?"

Mel could hear the faint sound of water running in the background. Her heart didn't want to believe it. Not after he promised he wanted to give them a try. Something felt wrong, but she didn't want to stick around any longer.

Her heart felt like it was being squeezed in her chest. The prickle of tears stung her eyes. She refused to cry in front of the fake bimbo. She willed her tears to hold off a few more minutes until she was in the privacy of her own apartment.

"No, I don't need any of your sloppy seconds. I hope you enjoyed the ride because he's never going to commit to you. You're just an easy lay when he's bored. But hey, who am I to judge? Some women are ok with being a revolving door."

Candace's smirk dropped. That gave Melanie a momentary sense of satisfaction. Melanie turned around and headed for the stairs not waiting for a response.

The next morning, Mel woke up earlier than normal. She hadn't really slept much to begin with. Constant tossing and turning kept her up half the night. It didn't add up. Sometime during the night, she decided that she was long overdue to visit her father. Every time they talked, he asked when she was going to visit.

She needed time to clear her head and to think about things with her and Skylar. A trip to her dad's house was long overdue. Sometimes a girl just needed her dad. She scrolled through her phone and booked a flight for the next day. She texted her boss to let her know that she was going to be out of town for a few days. She knew she wouldn't mind because Melanie never took time off.

She called her dad to tell him her flight information so he could pick her up. There was a text message from Skylar from the wee hours of the morning. Only a few hours after she'd found Candace in his apartment.

Skylar: I missed seeing you today. I hope you have sweet dreams; of me, of course.

There was a kissy heart emoji and one with a huge grin.

Even after last night, she couldn't help the chuckle that escaped. Leave it to Skylar to say something so big-headed. Melanie didn't reply to the message. She decided she wouldn't contact him until she touched down in Texas.

CHAPTER TWENTY-THREE

Melanie checked her phone as soon as she woke the next morning. There weren't any more text messages from Skylar. She shouldn't be surprised since it was only six. Her flight didn't leave until eleven, but she wanted to get to the airport early. That left less time to run into Skylar.

To help her wake up, she took a warm shower. She stood under the stream of hot water letting it massage her skin. Her thoughts were lost in what happened. She felt angry, sad, and stupid. The tears would follow if she dwelled on the sadness.

Fresh out of the shower and dressed in yoga pants and a v-neck t-shirt, she grabbed the suitcase she had packed. She texted Claudia and Jade to tell them she was going to be out of town and ask if they could check on her apartment. They didn't know about Candace yet. She was too embarrassed that she'd been played. Claudia didn't need the extra stress anyway. She had enough to worry about.

Melanie didn't bother to make coffee or breakfast. Airport breakfast would do for the day. She pulled up the Uber app on her phone and scheduled a ride. Both Claudia and Jade had offered to drive her, but she didn't want them to question why she was leaving so much earlier than her flight. There was an Uber not too far from her house, so she locked up her apartment and headed outside to wait.

Melanie's head was down scrolling through apps on her phone when her Uber pulled up. She was putting the phone back into her purse when she heard her name.

Oh no.

She knew whose voice it was before she looked up. Skylar was jogging toward her wearing a pair of running shorts and no shirt. His hair was damp from sweat and he looked as sexy as ever.

She'd forgotten that the man rarely slept in and ran every day. Jumping into the car to make a run for it wasn't a choice, so she stood there as he approached.

"Hey, if this isn't a good morning surprise," he smiled as he leaned in to kiss her.

Melanie backed away to avoid the kiss. Skylar's smile dropped and his eyebrows furrowed.

"What's wrong?"

When he noticed the car she was standing next to, he asked, "Where are you going?"

"I'm going to see my dad."

"Oookayy, why didn't you mention it before? Were you going to say bye?"

"It was a last-minute decision."

His face went from confusion to concern.

"Is everything ok? Is your dad ok? Do you need me to go with you?"

Melanie's heart melted at the tenderness in his voice. This was the Skylar that she knew and was falling for.

"Everything's fine. I just need a break."

"A break from what?"

"Everything."

"Talk to me, Mel. What's going on?"

He tried to reach out and touch her, but she flinched.

"You could ask Candace if you really don't know what's wrong."

"Candace? What does she have to do with anything?"

Maybe he really wasn't there last night. Had Candace gotten into his apartment without him knowing? Melanie felt so confused.

"Don't mess with me, Skylar. I don't like liars. Do you really not know what I'm talking about?"

"I have no idea. I'm starting to get angry because whatever it is has obviously upset you, but you won't tell me what it is."

The Uber driver rolled down his window. Melanie turned to see what he wanted.

"Miss, do you still need a ride?"

"Yes, I'm sorry I just need another minute."

The driver rolled the window back up and she turned to face Skylar. The concern on his face broke her. A few stray tears trickled down her cheek. Before she got a chance, Skylar's hand reached out to wipe them away. He reached for her to pull her into his arms and she let him. She didn't stay there long before she pushed away. She straightened up and wiped any remaining wetness with the back of her hand.

"I went to your apartment last night after I got home from Claudia's. I figured you always pop up at my place, so why not come and surprise you?" Skylar didn't say anything, just nodded his head and listened. "At first no one answered, so I figured you weren't home."

Then he did interrupt.

"I was at Brendon's last night. We had a poker night with some of the guys."

"Interesting, because Candace answered your door wearing nothing but her panties and one of your shirts. She looked rumpled and said that you were in the shower. I could hear the shower in the background."

Skylar's hands balled into fists at his side and he started to pace. His face was red and his lips turned into a deep scowl.

"Why didn't you call or text me? Did my text last night not give you any sign that I wasn't thinking about any other woman, let alone being with another woman? You're all I ever think about, Mel."

Melanie's gaze was on the ground.

"I don't know. She shocked me by being in your place. How'd she get in if you didn't let her in? I was mad and upset. I have to admit I was skeptical, but I didn't know what to think."

"I don't know how the hell she got into my apartment, but I'm sure as hell going to find out. You should have called me or tried to come back later when you thought I may be out of the shower. Instead, you're running away."

"I'm not running. I was going to talk to you once I got to Texas. I was thinking with my heart not my head. My feelings were hurt. You don't have the best track record with relationships, and I'm scared that you're going to ruin me. I just thought I needed some space and time to process things. I honestly need my dad right now."

Skylar stepped closer to Melanie. He cupped her face in his hands tilting her head back to look at him.

"You were trying to run, sweetheart, but I won't let you. I'll chase you and, believe me, I will catch you. I know I haven't been Mr. Relationship in the past, but you have to trust that I'm committed to us. People can change Mel, and you've helped change me."

Skylar bent down and placed a tender kiss on her lips. He didn't deepen the kiss like Melanie secretly hoped he would. He kissed her on her nose and her forehead then pulled her into a hug.

"I don't want you to go under these circumstances, but I understand if you need to visit your dad. Just know I'm not going anywhere. You should already know you can't get rid of me that easily. I'm going to get the bottom of this Candace thing and get rid of her once and for all."

Skylar loaded her bag into the car. She slid into the back seat. He reached in and gave her one last kiss before shutting the door. He waved as she pulled off. Before they turned out of the complex, she looked out of the back window. Skylar was still standing there watching her.

There were still doubts lurking in the back of her mind. She wanted to believe him, she did believe him, but she feared that Candace would be a constant interference in their relationship. She'd done a good job interfering up until that point. It was clear she would stop at nothing

CHAPTER TWENTY-FOUR

Skylar watched Melanie's Uber drive away. He cursed out loud at the whole situation. He'd found a girl that made him want to be better and Candace found a way to mess it up. He'd hoped that she had seriously backed off since he hadn't heard from her, but it was clear she had been scheming.

If he didn't step in, Candace would never stop. She seemed to think that if she couldn't have him, no one would. She had a personal vendetta against Melanie. Skylar scrolled through his contacts until he got to Brendon's number.

"What up, bro?"

"Nothing. Well, everything. I need your computer skills. I'll explain later."

"Okay, should I be concerned?"

"Nope, once you help me, all will be well."

"Alright then, I'll be over tonight."

Back in his apartment, Skylar started to brainstorm. He didn't want to play dirty, but Candace left him no choice. She forgot who she was messing with and how much she'd revealed about herself to him in private. Between him and Brendon, they could come up with a plan to get her to back off. He'd be nice enough to give her the option to walk away before he put her on blast to her parents. She wouldn't want them to know that their perfect little princess wasn't so perfect.

* * *

Melanie retrieved her bag from the baggage claim and headed outside to the pickup area to find her dad. It didn't take long to spot her old man. He was standing by a silver SUV. His once black hair was being taken over by gray. His large frame towered over Gwen who was nestled beside him. She always remembered her dad as being a big man. He always made her feel safe as a child. He still reminded her of the man that eased her fears as a child, but now he had slight wrinkles around his eyes and mouth.

As soon as her dad spotted her, he released Gwen and moved toward her. Father and daughter met in the middle. Melanie released the handle of her suitcase so she could be pulled into her dad's embrace. His strong arms wrapped around her shoulders. An instant comfort fell over her that only her dad could provide.

"I missed you so much," she mumbled into his shirt.

"I missed you too, sweetheart. So much. I'm so happy you're here."

Gwen came up beside her father and placed her hand on his arm.

"Robert, stop hogging her. I need a hug too." It was still always funny for Melanie to hear her dad called Wallace. When her mother was alive, she called him Bobby.

"Hey, Gwen, it's good to see you." Melanie moved from her father's embrace to Gwen's softer one.

"Mel, we're so happy you're here. It's been too long, dear."

The two women pulled apart.

"It has. I'm sorry it took me so long to visit."

"Oh, none of that. You're here now, and we are going to make the most of it."

Even though Gwen came into her life after she was an adult, Melanie liked having a motherly figure around. She was more like a friend than anything, but it was still nice to have an older and wiser woman's opinion sometimes.

Melanie's dad loaded her luggage into the trunk while the two women piled into the car. On the ride back to her dad's house, they talked about work, their garden, Mel's blog and other random things.

"Want to stop for lunch, honey? I'm sure you're hungry after all that travel."

"Sure, then I want to take a nap."

They decided on a small diner that her dad and Gwen frequented. The staff all knew them. Her dad introduced her to everyone like the proud father he was, and Melanie didn't stop his bragging. He was excited that his only child was there to visit. She wouldn't take his moment away.

After speaking to a dozen people, and filling up on the best country fried chicken Melanie had ever had, they headed home. As soon as they entered, Melanie felt a sense of home. It wasn't the home she grew up in, but it still gave her that sense of peace and comfort. She attributed it to the fact that home would always be where her father was. They had been their own little team for so long after her mom passed.

"I want to spend time with you guys, but I can barely keep my eyes open."

"That's ok, sweet pea. Go take a nap."

She gave her dad a kiss on the cheek before heading to the guest room. It was only a matter of minutes before she drifted off.

Two and a half hours later, she woke up feeling much more refreshed. She reached for her phone to check the time. She was surprised there was a text message from Skylar. If what he said was true, then she shouldn't be surprised.

Skylar: Did you make it to your dad's ok?

There was another one forty-five minutes later.

Skylar: I get that you're mad, but please at least tell me you're ok.

Mel considered not responding, but that would be mean.

Mel: I made it here. Just woke up from a nap.

Skylar: Glad you made it safe. I wish I were there to nap with you.

Dang him! Why did he have to be so sweet when she couldn't get her thoughts and feelings in order? She didn't bother replying. Instead, she climbed out of bed and headed to the bathroom. She splashed cold water on her face to help wake her up. Travel days always seemed to take it out of her.

Melanie made her way into the family room to look for her dad and Gwen. The family room was quiet. There were no sounds coming from the house at all. She wandered through the house until she found Gwen sitting in the sunroom with a book.

"Hey," she said from the doorway. "Where's Dad?"

"Hey, sleepy head. He ran out to get some stuff for dinner. He wants to cook out on the grill to celebrate your being here."

"Sounds good," Melanie said while settling into one of the chairs across from Gwen.

"How are things going in the Midwest?"

Melanie let her head relax back onto the chair.

"Oh, they're going I suppose. Work's good. I love my job. The blog is a work in progress, but good."

"I'm so glad to hear that. I try to check in on your blog every week. I've told the girls at my book club all about it. Many of them wish that you lived closer so that you could style them."

That comment sparked new ideas for her personal styling business. She tucked them into the back of her mind to explore later.

"I'd love to. Maybe one day, when my business grows, I'll be able to expand my reach."

"There'll be a list of eager clients for you here in Texas when you do."

"Thanks, Gwen." Melanie gave her stepmother a small smile.

"How's everything else going? Any new gentlemen?"

Melanie should have seen that coming. Her dad was itching for her to settle down and give him a few grandkids. Skylar popped into her mind. She didn't immediately push the thought away. That in itself scared her. She weighed her options of bringing Skylar up to Gwen. She desperately wanted to talk to someone about what had been going on. Gwen knew nothing about the situation and may give her a fresh perspective from Claudia and Jade.

"I have a new neighbor. Well, he isn't new anymore, but yeah. I have a neighbor."

Gwen sat her book beside her and leaned back in her seat.

"A neighbor, huh? We've all got neighbors, so there must be more to this neighbor than that."

"He's a pain my butt. He's also sweet and caring and protective."

"Ah, I see."

What did she see?

"Does this pain in the butt have a name?"

"Skylar."

"Does this Skylar have anything to do with why you're here?"

Melanie looked away ashamed that Gwen was right.

"Yes. No. Kinda. I was overdue for a visit, and I wanted to see you and dad. He just helped give me the extra push I needed."

"It's clear that there is more to this neighbor and, if you want to talk about it, I'll be glad to listen. If you want to wait and talk to your dad, I'm sure he will be glad to listen too."

Melanie had always talked to her dad about everything. They'd always been super close. She'd also grown to adore Gwen over the years. With that thought, she told Gwen all about how they met, his sister's wedding, and Candace.

"No wonder you needed a vacation. That Candace sounds like a real headache."

"That's putting it mildly."

"Do you care about Skylar, Mel?"

The man drove her crazy at times, always showing up unannounced, eating her food, cuddling with her on the couch, making her laugh.

"Yes."

"I'll let you in on a little secret. Love is hard. Relationships are hard. When your dad and I met, do you think it was love at first sight? For me maybe, but not for him. Your dad still loved your mother when I met him. He still does. Gradually, he was able to open his heart to the idea of loving someone else, and the understanding that it didn't mean that he'd loved your mother any less. I had to be very patient when it came to your father. We started out as friends. I always knew I wanted more, but I couldn't let on to him; he would have run like a wild alley cat."

"How did you stay so patient? How'd you know it would be worth it?"

"With the right person, love is always worth it. There will always be obstacles because that is life. If you have someone who's willing to work with you, and is devoted, then you can work through the tough stuff. It sounds like Skylar is all-in with you. Sure, the Candace girl is trying to come between you, but it seems to me like he's not letting her. He's been open and honest with you. It seems like he's putting in the work. Question is: are you willing to work with him?"

Melanie let Gwen's words sink in. Was she ready to work with him for what they could have? She hadn't felt the way she did with Skylar with anyone else. The ornery man had weaseled his way into being one of her best friends. Her thoughts were interrupted when Gwen spoke again.

"Has he tried to contact you since you've been here?"

"Yes, he texted me as soon as I got here. He's sent me a few more since, but I haven't really replied."

"You youngins and your text messaging. You can't always say everything you need to in a text. Sounds like you have a phone call to make, sweetie. Don't make the man wait. Heck, don't make yourself wait."

Melanie stood up and stretched her body out. She walked over to Gwen and bent down to give her a hug.

"Thanks, Gwen. I'm glad you were patient with my dad. We're really lucky to have you."

* * *

There was an obnoxious knock on Skylar's front door around six that evening. He knew it was Brendon; not because he asked him over, but because Brendon always knocked to the beat of whatever song was in his head.

"Can't you knock like a normal person?" Skylar asked when he opened the door for his brother.

"Nope, I can't help it when I feel the beat."

"Whatever, man Get in here so you can help me."

Skylar went to the kitchen and grabbed two beers while Brendon made himself at home on the couch.

"What was so pressing that I had to come over tonight?"

"Candace."

"I thought you guys were over. You better not be playing Mel. You're my bro, but I like Mel. I'll have to beat you up to defend her honor."

Skylar threw one of the pillows from the couch at his brother's head.

"No, doofus. Candace is still causing problems. She broke into my apartment and pretended we'd just had sex. Mel came to see me and Candace answered the door in my shirt and her underwear."

"Dude, how the hell did she get into your apartment?"

"I have no idea. I plan on finding out though. I want to use some dirt on her to make her back off. She'd hate for Mommy and Daddy to find out that their perfect angel isn't so perfect."

"So you want to blackmail her?"

"I prefer to call it assisting her in making sound decisions."

"Sounds classy."

"I thought so. I need your help because we may need to get into her e-mail or Facebook or something to get some evidence. I know you're basically a hacker so yeah."

"I'm not a hacker. I just know how to find the things I need when I need them."

"Whatever helps you sleep at night, bro."

"I think I know what you can use for your little plan."

"What?"

"Landon told me about something very interesting he saw at the wedding. Something that I'm sure Little Miss Home Wrecker wouldn't want her parents to know."

Skylar moved to the edge of his seat. "Do tell, bro, do tell."

CHAPTER TWENTY-FIVE

Melanie was sitting against the headboard of the bed in the guest room. She pulled up Skylar's number for what felt like the hundredth time. In reality, it had only been twenty. Gwen's advice to call him was sound. It didn't make it any easier. Getting hurt was not on her list of things to do, and she feared that it was inevitable with Candace in the picture.

Melanie took in a deep breath, closed her eyes and made her finger hit the call button. Her breaths came faster and sharper as the phone rang. Just when she started to hang up, the ringing stopped.

"Mel?"

She squeezed closed eyes.

"Yeah." She slapped her hand against her head; so much for playing it cool.

"Hey, how' your visit with your dad going? I miss you."

Dear Lord, her heart about beat out of her chest hearing those words uttered from him. She'd missed him too; so much.

"It's going really well. I can tell that he's happy that I'm here."

"Good to hear." Melanie heard a laugh in the background and instantly recognized it as Brendon.

"Brendon's there? Tell my buddy I say hello."

Skylar made a psh sound. "I'm not wasting my talk time with you relaying messages to my younger, less handsome brother."

Melanie couldn't hold back the belly laugh that burst from her. This was exactly what she liked about Skylar and was one of the many things she had missed about seeing and talking to him every day. She heard Brendon in the background stating his argument as to why he was the better looking Stillman brother. Her lips stayed in a smile long after she stopped giggling.

"I missed your laugh," Skylar whispered.

Melanie hugged her knees into her chest. Sinking a little deeper into the bed.

"I've missed you too."

"Do you know when you'll be coming home?" There was some relief in his voice.

"Probably in a few days. I don't have my return ticket yet."

"Do you want me to pick you up from the airport when you get back?"

"We'll see."

Skylar made a sound in reply.

"Hey, Mel, I'm really sorry about the whole Candace thing. Brendon and I were coming up with a plan to get rid of her. I don't want her coming between us anymore. I want you to be secure in us; in me."

Melanie squeezed the phone in her hand. She wanted those same things.

"Do you trust me, Mel?"

Despite everything that had gone on with Candace, she did. When Candace opened the door to Skylar's apartment, she'd felt that there was no way it was real; but it was so inexplicable at the time.

"Yes," was all she replied, but that was all Skylar needed.

"Thank you, Mel. Your trust means so much to me. I promise you that, by the time you come home, the situation with Candace will be handled.

* * *

"Are you sure this is going to work?" Skylar paced back and forth across Brendon's living room.

"Bro, sit down. You're making me nervous. It's going to work. Candace cares about three things: money, status, and men. You threaten to take any of those things away and she'll fold. Trust me."

Skylar ran his hands through his hair before placing them on his hips. He turned his gaze back to Brendon. "What if she figures out that there are cameras?"

Brendon got up from the couch and walked to his brother. He placed his hands on his shoulders and gave him a little shake. "Come on, bro. She isn't that smart. Even if she was, she isn't very observant. She can't even take the hint that you don't want her. The cameras are obscure. You wouldn't even know they were there if you weren't there when I set them up."

Skylar dropped his face into his hands. "You're right. Okay, I'm just ready to get this over with."

Brendon turned Skylar toward the door and began to guide him. "You need to get going so you can be there when she arrives. Just keep your cool, and remember to get her to admit to everything."

Less than twenty minutes later, Skylar was back at his own place pacing. He straightened the couch cushions every two minutes. He kept checking all the places they'd hidden the tiny cameras. Who knew there were cameras that small?

A few light raps at his door made him jump. It was show time, and his nerves were ever present. He tried to suppress the feeling. If Candace sensed that anything was up, it could blow the whole thing. He wiped his hands on his pants and made his way to the door. Turning the doorknob, he plastered on the biggest, most fake smile he could muster.

Before Skylar could say a word, Candace threw her arms around his neck. She tried to go in for a kiss, but he was fast enough to turn his head. He had to play a part, but there was no way he was letting her kiss him. Mel's lips were the only ones he wanted and he wouldn't betray her even for this.

"Sky-Sky, I'm so happy you came to your senses. I've missed you."

"Oh yeah?" Skylar tried to keep his answer vague.

Candace waltzed past him and sat in the middle of the couch. She patted the seat next to her.

"Come sit down. Let's talk and catch up."

Skylar walked slowly into the room. Instead of sitting on the couch he sat in the recliner he always sat in to watch T.V. Well, he always sat in it before Melanie. Now they cuddled up on the couch together. He had a sudden need to make Candace get off of his couch. He suppressed the feeling and tried to focus on the task at hand.

Candace's face formed a pout when she realized that Skylar wasn't going to sit by her.

"Candace, tell me what have you been up to?" Skylar leaned forward in the chair propping his chin on his hand. He feigned interest in whatever it was she was about to say.

"Ugh, I've been so busy. Work has been a nightmare. They tried to get me to work overtime, but I had nail and hair appointments. Then I had a massage on Thursday. I didn't have time to work more hours. It's just been so hectic."

Skylar swore his eyelids drifted closed listening to Candace.

"Made any house calls lately?"

"House calls? We don't do that kind of stuff. Clients have to come to us."

Skylar sat up straighter in his chair.

"That's funny because Mel told me she happened to stop by my house the other day. I wasn't here but, oddly enough, someone answered my door. I don't remember inviting anyone over or giving anyone a key to my place."

He saw the color drain from Candace's face. She tried to school her features, but her whole body turned rigid.

"Wow, you should really talk to your landlord about that. You can never be too safe." Candace's eyes looked around the room like she was trying to find a secret escape route. Her eyes refused to meet Skylar's.

"Cut the crap, Candace. You were in my apartment. What I don't know is why; or how you got in here. I also can't understand why you pretended like I was here, and that we'd had sex, when I told you I was done a long time ago."

Candace stood up from her place on the couch. She walked over to Skylar trying to sit on his lap. Skylar stood and placed his hands in front of him to keep her at a distance.

"Whoa, whoa, back up. I'm trying to be civil about this. Don't push me, Candace."

Candace crossed her arms over her chest and took a defensive stance. She finally looked like she understood that Skylar wasn't joking.

"Fine, I was here. I copied your house key a while ago. At the time, I did it in case I ever wanted to surprise you with sexy-time. I just can't see why you would want to be with her when you can have me."

Skylar moved until he was standing right in front of her staring eye to eye.

"It's none of your business who I see. What you need to do is get it through your thick skull that we are done. Don't compare yourself to Mel. She isn't self-centered like you. I don't know what to say about the key other than you are truly insane."

Candace jutted her chin out and stuck her nose in the air.

"I'd say you're the one that's insane. When you can have me over her, you have to be crazy. I'd rather be crazy than look like her."

"Like what?... Beautiful, feminine?"

"Whatever. You're clearly delusional."

"I'm not delusional. In fact, a little birdy told me that you and Mr. Donovan got a little up close and personal at Sam's wedding. I wonder how your mom would feel about you sleeping with her best friend's husband."

Candace took several steps away from Skylar. Her jaw dropped open at his revelation. Her reaction alone was all the evidence he needed, but he had to have her verbally admit to the accusation.

"Who told you that?" she asked in a hushed voice.

"Does it really matter?"

"Yes, it matters because it's a complete lie!" Candace's voice trembled as it rose an octave.

"From the sounds I was told you were making, it didn't sound like a lie to me. We both know how loud you can be." Skylar cringed on the inside at his last statement, but he needed to solidify his case.

"Ahhhhh, son of a!" Candace's calm facade was gone. "So what does it matter if I did? What does it matter to you? He's the cheater; not me. He's the one stepping out on his wife. If she kept herself up and gave him what he needed, he wouldn't need me."

Skylar perched on the arm of the recliner. He was pleased that she was so quick to admit everything.

"Oh Candace, Candace, Candace. It doesn't matter one bit to me who you sleep with. You can sleep with every man in the city for all I care. I do, however, think that your mother might care."

"What the hell, Skylar? You can't tell my mom. I'll deny it, anyway. She would never take your word over mine."

"I don't need her to take my word for it. She can take yours."

Candace let out a humorless laugh. "As if I'm going to admit any of this to my mother."

"You don't have to. I have you on tape admitting to it. I can tell her for you."

Candace's eyes were wide. In an instant, she was in front of him grabbing his arms and shaking him.

"You're taping me? That's illegal, Skylar. I'll send you to jail."

"Breaking and entering is illegal too." He peeled her hands from his arms. He stood up from the chair's arm and looked down at her. "Go sit down."

Much to his surprise, she obeyed.

"This is what's going to happen. You're going to leave me and Mel alone. I want to build a relationship with her, and I can't do that with you playing your little games. You won't contact me. You will not speak to Melanie. You won't come to any of my family's functions. You can come down with the flu, have a work function, get the plague; I don't care. Just don't show up. If you fail to do these things, I will tell your parents that their perfect little princess is a home wrecker. I'd also be glad tell Mrs. Donovan that you've been helping her husband with his manly needs. The ones that she 'can't fulfill'." Skylar made sure to use air quotes when he said the last bit.

Candace shot off of the couch. She snatched her purse and stomped to the door. Yanking it open, she turned to him right outside of the threshold.

"Screw you, Skylar. I didn't want you, anyway. My mom kept pressuring me to be with you. You can have your stupid girlfriend. You'll regret this, and it will be too late."

"The only thing I regret is wasting time on you. Thanks for the ride, but it's over now." With that, Skylar shut the door in her face. He clicked the lock in place and made a mental note to get it changed.

CHAPTER TWENTY-SIX

Skylar called Melanie as soon as Candace left. He explained everything from Candace confessing about the affair with Mr. Donavan to breaking into his house. He'd even offered to let her listen to the recordings that they'd captured, but she'd refused.

She said she believed him, and that she was happy that Candace was out of the picture. The best part of the conversation was when she told him she'd be coming home in two days and she'd appreciate if he would pick her up from the airport. He fist pumped the air in excitement.

He couldn't wait to see her. He'd missed her more than he knew was possible. The inability to get a good night's sleep and irritability were living proof. He'd never cared about anyone, other than his parents and siblings, enough to miss them when they were gone. With Melanie, he couldn't wait to wrap his arms around her and devour her lips as soon as he saw her.

He had some planning to do and two days wasn't a lot of time. He set straight to work as soon as they hung up. Melanie deserved the best, and he was going to show her that he could give her that.

* * *

The seatbelt light above her head flashed indicating that it was time to buckle up. The pilot came over the intercom confirming that they would be landing soon. Melanie buckled herself in and turned to look out of the window. The clouds were so white and delicate. She wished she could reach out and run her hands through them just to know what they felt like.

Her mind began to wander to Skylar. It had only been a week and a half since she'd seen him, but it felt like much longer. She was both excited and nervous. Things had changed so much between them since they'd first met. She'd never imagined that he would be a friend, let alone her boyfriend. It still seemed weird when she thought about it.

She'd been happy when he told her about Candace. She'd known that there was no way Skylar would have been in the apartment that day, but sometimes insecurity could get the best of a person. She was ready to get back and start with a fresh slate. Who knew where things would go from there?

Thirty minutes later, Melanie was at baggage claim waiting for her bag. She saw her bright pink and yellow bag coming around and prepared to grab it. But before she had a chance, someone was snatching it off of the carousel.

"Hey-" she began to protest when she turned and her words caught in her throat.

Standing next to her, with his hand still on her bag, was Skylar. He was giving her the most adorable smile.

"Miss me?" he asked setting her bag down beside him.

"I see you're still as modest as ever. How'd you even get that big head of yours to fit in the doors?" Melanie returned his smile with one of her own.

"Gosh, I missed you," he said as he pulled her into his arms and kissing her right there beside baggage claim.

Melanie's body melted into his. P.D.A. was not her thing, but the fact that he wasn't afraid to stake his claim on her in the middle of the airport was all kinds of sexy.

Pulling away from her, he looked down into her eyes.

"Ready to go home?"

"Yep, definitely ready."

On the way to their apartment building, Melanie told Skylar all about her visit with her dad. He asked questions about her dad and Gwen. He wanted to know what they were like, if her dad had any hobbies, what he did for a living. He seemed genuinely interested in getting to know more about her dad. He even mentioned going with her next time she went to visit. She knew that it would be a while down the road, but it made her happy to know that he was thinking of them together long-term.

Melanie sighed in relief when they pulled into a parking spot. She had enjoyed the time with her dad, but she was glad to be home. Skylar pulled her suitcase from the trunk, and they headed inside. On the elevator ride to her floor, Skylar pulled her to him and placed small kisses down her jaw and neck. A shiver ran through her, and she felt her body responding to his touch.

The elevator door opened to her floor. He released her and gestured for her to step out in front of him. Before putting her key into the door, she looked over her shoulder and caught Skylar staring at her butt.

"Stare much?"

Skylar's eyes flicked up to meet hers.

"Just admiring my assets," he said with a smile.

"Yours?"

"Oh, yes; mine all mine."

Melanie shook her head and turned to unlock her door. A secret smile took over her lips. Dang if she didn't love hearing him say those words. Melanie opened her door and stepped aside so Skylar could carry her bag in.

"You can just leave it by the door. I'll get it later," she said as she made her way into the living room.

She stopped when she reached the entrance to the living room. Sitting on the table was a bouquet of two-dozen red roses and a bottle of her favorite sparkling drink. Propped against the bottle was an envelope.

Skylar's front was now flush against her back. She could feel the rhythm of his breathing.

"Go open the card." She felt his breath on his ear.

She walked over to the table and bent down to inhale the scent of the roses. She picked up the envelope and carefully opened it. On the front, there were two birds with their beaks touching like they were kissing. Inside, there was a cute little greeting card message. Under that in Skylar's writing it said:

'Mel,

Please join me this evening at six p.m. for dinner and entertainment. If you so choose to accompany me, please check your bedroom for further instructions.

-Skylar'

Melanie held the card to her chest and turned to Skylar. "The flowers are beautiful. What happens if I accept your invitation?"

"You have to go to your room to find out."

Eagar to see what was in store, she went to her room. She flipped the light switch and light flooded the room. Mel's eyes went straight to the bed and its contents. Lying there was a red bodycon dress and strappy black heels. Next to it, there was a pink Victoria's secret bag. She walked over and peeked into the bag. Her cheeks heated when she saw what was inside.

Skylar's arms snaked around her from behind. His chin settled on her shoulder. "Do you like it?"

"It's all so gorgeous. How did you know what to get? How did you even get into my house?"

"I had two little helpers that were more than willing to assist me."

Melanie turned in Skylar's arms to face him. She wrapped her arms around his neck and tilted her head back to look into his eyes.

"I should have known. My friends are always in my business."

"They just care about you and want to see you happy."

Skylar bent down and pressed another kiss to her lips. "So, do you accept my invitation for a date?"

Melanie brought her hand to her chin and pretended to be in deep thought. "Hmmm, I don't know. I have a whole bottle of my favorite drink and loads of Netflix documentaries on standby."

"I can assure you that our date will be ten times better than any documentary you will watch. I'll be sure to make it worth your while."

"Fine.. You drive a hard bargain."

"I typically get what I want, and there is nothing I want more than to spend tonight with you."

"I'd like that too."

Skylar took her hand and lead her to the en suite bathroom. On the counter, there was a basket full of bath bombs, body washes, body butter, and bubble baths.

"Oh my goodness, Skylar. This is too much."

"It will never be too much. If anything, it's not enough. I want you to be able to pamper yourself and relax before our evening."

'This is enough stuff to pamper me for months."

"Even better," he said. "Go ahead and get in. I'll lock the door on my way out. Just be ready when I come knocking at six sharp."

With a smack on her butt, he left her to it.

Melanie three-way called Jade and Claudia while she soaked in a tub overflowing with bubbles. They confirmed their part in helping Skylar but wouldn't give her any hints as to what the night held. Claudia told her to give up the P while Jade told her to enjoy being pampered and wooed.

At six pm, as promised, there was a knock on the door. Melanie hurried to the door and swung it open. Skylar was there in black slacks, a white shirt under a gray blazer, and a red tie. He looked edible. Melanie looked him up and down. Her tongue ran over her lips in appreciation.

"Don't do that, woman, or we won't make it out of here." Skylar stepped forward and pulled her into him placing a quick kiss on her lips.

"What if I don't want to make it out?" Her voice was breathy.

Skylar looked her in the eyes for several moments. His feelings for her were overwhelming.

"I'd love to stay here and explore every inch of your body in every room of this apartment, but we've got places to be."

Melanie poked out her bottom lip in a faux pout. Inside, she felt giddy that Skylar was going through all the trouble to take her out.

"I promise that we will have plenty of time for me to ravish you and break in your apartment. Let's get going, shall we?"

Skylar offered her his elbow. She smiled up at him. He had pulled out all the stops so far, and she couldn't wait to see what the night held.

In the car, Melanie resumed her normal control of the radio. Skylar let out a loud, over the top sigh when she began singing along to the terrible pop song that blared through the speaker.

"I have to remind myself that I signed up for these constant imitation Pop Princess renditions of awful pop songs."

Melanie side eyed him and gave his thigh a playful snack. His face broke out into a huge grin.

"Don't worry, I still love ya. I don't hold it against you. You have many other respectable talents."

Melanie went still in her seat. She knew her ears weren't playing tricks on her... were they? Maybe he meant like a friend. He didn't say 'I love you', he said 'I love ya'. Friends said that to each other all the time. She turned to look out at the night sky. She thought about her feelings for Skylar. If he did mean he loved her, did she love him too? The answer came easier than she had expected. Of course she loved him. No one puts up with someone who steals their food and constantly invites themselves over without loving them. Despite their rough start, her life had been much easier and more enjoyable since he'd entered it.

She was pulled from her thoughts when his hand reached and grabbed her smaller one.

"Whatcha thinking?"

Not wanting to talk about such a heavy topic, Melanie went with a safe topic. "I'm wondering where we are going."

"Wonder no longer. We're here."

Melanie looked up and saw they had stopped in front of an upscale restaurant downtown. A man in a black suit approached Skylar's side of the car and Skylar stepped out before handing the man his keys. Melanie followed suit, and a man dressed identically to the first one helped her out of the car. Then Skylar was there taking her hand and leading her to the door of the restaurant. He stopped right outside and pulled her into him for a kiss. It was brief, but it was full of promise and unspoken words.

Melanie pressed her hand to her lips. "What was that for?"

"I didn't think I needed a reason to kiss my woman. I'm just happy. Happier than I ever thought I'd be."

"Me too," Melanie whispered.

The inside of the place was so elegant. Melanie had never been to a place so nice. The lighting was dim and everything seemed to be made of bold, dark stained wood. The tables were lined with table clothes and equipped with proper place settings and wine glasses. There was artwork painted on the ceiling. It was gorgeous. They sat and looked over the menu. Melanie had some sticker shock with the prices, but Skylar assured her not to worry. He threatened that if she tried to order the cheapest thing on the menu, that he would order everything on the menu.

Melanie didn't order the cheapest thing, but it still felt like Skylar ordered so much food. He ordered two appetizers, they both got entrées, and he ordered a few extra sides for them to try and topped it off with dessert.

Melanie groaned when they had finally finished eating and the server walked away with the check and Skylar's card.

"You may have to roll me out of here. Everything was so good, and I am stuffed."

"I'd be glad to carry you out of here," Skylar winked at her.

"You aren't carrying me anywhere, crazy-pants."

"Fine, but the night isn't over."

"It's not? You've already done so much. What more could we possibly do?"

"I guess you'll see."

The server came back with Skylar's card and he squared away the bill. He stood up and shoved his wallet into his back pocket and then offered his hand to help her up. Skylar led them out of the restaurant and onto the busy downtown sidewalk. Melanie craned her neck to look up and around at the surrounding skyscrapers.

Skylar placed his hand on her lower back and started to lead her toward the street. When she focused her attention on what they were walking toward, she gasped. There was a horse with a white carriage attached. The carriage had white Christmas style lights lining the outside.

"Oh, Skylar; I can't believe it. This is seriously like something straight from a fairy-tale. I didn't know you had it in you."

Skylar's arm was wrapped around her waist and he had her pulled to his side. He looked down at her and kissed her forehead.

"Somehow, you bring the best out of me."

The man in charge of the ride helped Melanie into the carriage. Once she was settled in, Skylar followed close after. They rode along for several blocks with Melanie pointing out different buildings and businesses she'd never seen before. Skylar's arm was securely around her shoulder the whole time with his hand rubbing absently up and down her arm.

Skylar pulled his phone from his pocket and turned on the music mix he'd made for the evening. As the melody of the first song played, he placed his hand on her chin and turned her face to his. They sat looking into each other's eyes for several minutes.

Skylar wiped the hand that wasn't wrapped around Mel on his pant leg. He looked away from Melanie for a moment to gather his thoughts. When he looked back, he saw some uncertainty in her eyes. He was doing this all wrong. His nervous vibes were freaking her out. He could tell.

He took her hand into his, took a deep breath, and began to speak.

"Melanie, things have been insane since I first met you. I thought we were going to be archenemies, but you've surprised me. I look forward to seeing you every day. I love how you always cook enough food for me even though you swear that you made extra for your lunch. I love how you are a little sparkling cider addict. I love how, when we watch T.V., you curl your cold little toes under me to keep warm. You are my best friend, and I love everything about you, Mel. I love you, Melanie."

Skylar felt like he hadn't taken a breath since starting his little speech. He took a breath then held it waiting to see what she said. He'd never told any woman besides his mom and Sam that he loved them. He'd never loved any other woman.

Melanie's eyes were glassy, and Skylar was afraid for a moment until her hands were on either side of his face and she was pulling him into a kiss. Her tongue plunged into his mouth to caress his. She let out a little moan before pulling back, not releasing his face, and looking into his eyes.

"I love you so much, Skylar. I was scared when I started to fall for you, but my heart didn't care. It went ahead and fell. I'm so glad it did."

Skylar pulled her back into him and reclaimed her lips. His mouth was more assertive now. He took control of the kiss, moving his lips from her mouth down to her neck. He made his way down to her breast. They were on perfect display in the dress and his pants grew tight just thinking about it. His hands moved up to cup her breast through her dress. Her nipples were pebbled and ready for any attention he was willing to give them.

"Skylar," her voice was low.

"You are so beautiful, Melanie."

He grabbed her hand and led it to the bulge in his pants. They had fooled around some during their late night movie sessions, but nothing ever went much past kissing and the ol' high school feel-up. Tonight, Skylar knew that those things wouldn't be enough. He needed her; all of her.

"This is what you do to me. You make me crazy. Do you know how many times I've got myself off thinking about you? How many cold showers I had to take while you waited for me on the couch to start a movie? A whole hell of a lot."

Mel's breaths were labored. She felt the telltale sign of wetness between her legs. She squeezed her legs together trying to ease the throbbing.

"Skylar, we can't do this here. There are people everywhere."

He huffed and slowly sat back in his seat. He adjusted his pants, which had become increasingly uncomfortable.

"You're right. I think maybe we should end this date early."

Forty-seven minutes; that's how long it took before they pulled into their parking lot. Skylar knew because he'd been counting them. They made their way into the building and into the elevator without a word. Skylar didn't bother pushing the button to his floor. They went straight to hers. He didn't want to take her to the place where he and Candace had been together. The thought reminded him that he needed to burn that bed.

When they got to her floor, Skylar took Melanie's keys from her hands. He opened the door and gestured for her to step in. He clicked the locks into place and turned to her. Her back was to him and she'd just taken off her shoes and was setting her purse on the entryway table.

Moving up behind her, he slid his hands under the hem of her dress. Melanie's breath caught as his hands slid over her ass. He gently rubbed and squeezed, loving that she had more than a handful. He couldn't wait to bend her over and see it in all of its glory.

His right hand reached around her and dipped below her panty line. Melanie started to rub her backside against his erection. It felt so good that he thought he might get off just from that feeling alone. He held her tight to him to slow down the torment of her gyrating hips.

His finger ran over her slit and the sexiest moan fell from her lips.

"You're so wet," he said as he flicked his finger over her nub. Skylar got the reaction he'd hoped for. "All this just for me? It must be my lucky day," he teased as his lips skimmed her neck and he licked and nipped at her ear.

"Skylar, please."

"Please what? Tell me what you want, baby." He continued to run his finger over her clit.

"I need you. I want you inside of me. Now."

Skylar turned her to face him. "Oh, we'll get there, but there's no way I'm doing anything before I get to taste you."

He didn't wait for her reply. He bent down, placed his arm around her thighs and carried her over his shoulder to her bedroom.

"Put me down, you oaf!"

"Hey, that's no way to talk to the man that's going to make you scream his name. I'm going to put you down as soon as we get to your room."

No sooner had he finished his sentence, than they entered her room. He flipped her off his shoulder, and she bounced on the bed. He stood at the end of the bed with his eyes on her. Slowly, he removed his tie and then unbuttoned his shirt. Mel watched him in a daze.

She was pulled out of her daze when Skylar grabbed onto her ankles and gently pulled her to the end of the bed. He kneeled down in front of her and lifted the skirt of her dress.

"My second dessert," he mumbled as he hooked his fingers on either side of her panties and pulled them down her legs.

Skylar ran his hands up and down her thighs before kissing his way from the inside of her knee to her inner thigh. He kissed his way up until he reached his prize. He kissed her seam and jutted his tongue out to lick her nub. Melanie's hips bucked off of the bed and rose toward him..

Loving the reaction he got, Skylar licked and sucked slowly before picking up the pace as her body squirmed on the bed. Her breaths were getting heavier and her moans louder with each pass of his tongue. Skylar reached down and began to stroke his shaft.

"Skylar, ahhhhhh." Melanie had a large intake of breath before she shattered completely. "Yeeeeeeesss!" Her hips continued to buck with every stroke of his tongue riding out the best orgasm she'd had; ever.

Skylar grabbed his wallet and pulled out the condom he'd placed in there before leaving the house earlier. He'd hoped that the night would end in lovemaking. It truly was his lucky day. He made quick work of undoing his pants and kicking them off. Pulling Melanie to a sitting position, he gently pulled her dress over her head and threw it on top of his pants. Her bra was next. He eased her back down on the bed and propped himself up above her on his arms. He captured her nipple in his mouth. He went back and forth rubbing and licking each hard peak.

When her moans became too much for him to bear, he positioned himself between Melanie's thighs. He rolled the condom from his wallet onto his length and then gripped her hips while gazing into her eyes. Leaning down, he placed a kiss on her already kiss-swollen lips. Skylar slowly pushed inside of her. Once he was all the way in, he closed his eyes and savored the feel.

"So perfect," he murmured.

He pulled back out and, slowly, slid himself back in. He kept up at a slow, agonizing pace until Melanie spoke up.

"I need you Skylar. Please. I feel like I'm going to die if you don't go faster."

Before she knew what was happening, Skylar flipped her over onto her stomach. He pulled her back toward him and lifted her backside until her soft, round behind was level with his hips . He positioned himself at her opening and pushed in without hesitation. He pulled out and thrust back in rapid succession.

"Skylar, that feels so good."

Skylar ran one hand through her hair and pulled her head back to him. He kissed the sensitive spot behind her ear while one of his hands reached around to play with her clit.

"I'm coming! Ooooh, Skylar!"

Melanie called out his name as she moaned, her cries lasting almost as long as the orgasm that shot through her body like electricity causing her to tremble with its force.

Skylar kept his pace. He felt himself coming close to the edge just as Melanie screamed his name. That's all it took for him to release, and then the two of them collapsed on the bed. They lay there for several minutes holding onto one another and trying to catch their breath.

"Best sex ever," Mel said with a sexy smile.

"Ditto," Skylar replied. "There will be lots more where that came from."

"I sure hope so because if I wasn't addicted to you before, I definitely am now."

"I'm glad because now that you've confessed your undying love for me, you're mine for keeps."

"You are so full of it, Skylar, but I do love you; ego and all.

EPILOGUE

"Babe, can you please shut up? I love you, but you can't hit the same notes as Whitney."

Melanie gave Skylar the stink eye and crossed her arms over her chest.

"I'm telling your mom on you as soon as we get there. Sam and I are her favorites."

Skylar removed one hand from the steering wheel and placed it on the back of her neck. He gently began to massage.

"I know. You make sure to remind me whenever you get the chance, love."

"You'd do good not to forget it, sweetums," she said in a dry tone.

No matter how long they were together, they still went back and forth. They gave as good as they got. Skylar pulled into his parent's long driveway. They were staying there for the weekend for a big birthday bash Skylar's mom was throwing for his dad. As Skylar was opening the car door for Melanie, his mom came out of the front door and made her way toward them.

"Hey, Mom," Skylar said preparing to envelop her into a hug.

"Hi, sweetie. Mel, darling you look lovely," his mom wrapped Melanie into a hug ignoring his outstretched arms.

"Thank you; it's so good to see you."

The two women pulled apart and his mother took Melanie's arm leading her into the house. They were babbling about some new clothing line or something that Melanie had blogged about. Skylar watched the two women disappear into the house and shook his head. You'd think they hadn't just seen each other last week. Skylar's dad, who'd followed his wife outside, came up and gave his son a pat on the back.

"Mom just ignored me and stole my girl."

"This is your future, son. Just be happy they get along."

Skylar grumbled something under his breath as he got their bags from the trunk.

"You ready for this, son?"

"As ready as I can be. I've never been more sure of anything in my life. I honestly didn't think I'd ever see this day."

"I always knew you would. It just took the right woman to bring you to your knees."

Skylar laughed thinking about how Mel kept him on his toes and never let his cocky ways faze her. She didn't chase after him like most women he'd dated. If you could even call what he'd done in the past dating. She definitely brought him to his knees, and he loved the sounds she made when she did.

"She brought me to my knees alright. When I least expected it, too."

The two men walked into the house to find their ladies.

The family was set to have a quiet family dinner that night. Arabella was making a feast that seemed way too much for them, but with all her kids and their significant others there, Mel figured she wanted leftovers.

"Hey, Mel, want to run into town with me to pick up some last minute stuff we need for Dad's party? We'll be back before dinner," Sam asked Melanie who was sitting at the kitchen island talking to Arabella.

"Sure, I'm down to ride. At least with you I can listen to good music without complaint. Your brother is a total baby."

"I heard that," Skylar yelled from the family room. The men were in the family room having a few beers while they waited for dinner.

Melanie and Sam made their way to town. They started at a large party store to get balloons, a sign, napkins, and other odds and ends. The second stop was a local superstore to get fruit and veggie trays for people to munch on. They got distracted by the beauty aisles looking at makeup and nail polish. The two both walked out with way more makeup than they needed, but they were secretly addicts.

"I hope your mom doesn't kill us for taking so long. We've been gone for three hours, Sam."

"Eh, she knew what she was doing when she sent the two of us to do her shopping," Sam said giggling.

"You make a good point," Melanie laughed.

Thirty minutes later, they arrived back at the Stillmans' residence. Both women loaded their arms with bags and carried them into the kitchen. The house was oddly quiet. Melanie assumed they were all either outside or in their rooms getting ready for dinner. They made quick work of putting their purchases away.

"I better put this makeup in my room and see if I can find Sky."

Sam walked over to her and grabbed the bag from her sitting it on the island. "Let's grab a drink and go out back. You can take that upstairs later."

Melanie agreed and Sam poured them both a glass of wine and led the way to the patio. As they got closer to the patio door, Melanie immediately thought something was wrong. It was pitch black, but there were small flickers of light reflecting on the door.

"Is there a fire out there?" she asked.

"No, silly," Sam laughed as they reached the door. She turned and grabbed Melanie's glass before opening it.

"Hey," Melanie started and then her voice caught in her throat.

There was Skylar right in front of her; on one knee. The fire she saw were small candles lit and placed around the patio. Behind Skylar was a group of people. Her eyes scanned the group: Claudia, Jade, Brendon...

"Dad?"

He gave her a small wave and was smiling from ear to ear. "Hey, baby girl."

Melanie's eyes dropped back to Skylar who was smiling, but she could tell it was a little strained. He was nervous.

"Melanie, come here, sweetheart."

Thankfully, her feet moved on their own because she wasn't able to think.

Skylar reached up for her hand. He turned her palm over and placed a kiss on it, and then placed the same hand to his heart. Melanie felt that familiar burn that came before tears. Her throat felt like it was clogged. She tried to swallow past it and hold back the flood gates.

"To say we got off to a rocky start would be putting it nicely. You accused me of having no manners. You didn't want to accept my help when I offered it. I was sure you were going to be a constant thorn in my side." There was laughter and love in his eyes as he continued his speech. "While you still try to damage my hearing every time we get into the car, and sometimes in the shower, I wouldn't trade my time with you for anything. At the chance of sounding cliché, you made me want to be a better person. I am a better person because I know you; because I get to love and be loved by you. If I have to do life with anyone, I want it to be with you. Melanie, will you marry me?"

Tears were streaming down her face. She started to nod her head 'yes'.

"I need you to say it, Mel."

"Yes. Yes, I'll marry you."

Skylar slid the ring onto her proper finger. Standing up, he wrapped her in a hug and lifted her off of the ground. Melanie buried her face in his neck.

"I can't believe you got my dad here," she whispered.

He squeezed her a little tighter. "I knew how important it would be to you for him to be here."

"I love you, Skylar Stillman."

"I love you too, future Mrs. Stillman."

"I like the sound of that."

When he put her down, she grabbed his face and pulled him down for a kiss. When they pulled away, they both had goofy grins on their faces.

"One question; Can I sing at our wedding?"

"Not a chance."

About the Author

Lanee Lane is a long time avid romance reader. Growing up her mother had bookcases full of romance novels. One book and she was hooked. She enjoys reading about all types of romance, but her favorites feature curvy heroines and the men that love them.

Lanee lives in the Midwest, where it's way too cold in the winter, with her husband and dog Bernie. She enjoys Zumba, well any kind of dance really, playing in makeup, and she may have a slight obsession with The Office.

You can connect with her on her Facebook page at:
https://Facebook.com/laneeslane
To keep up to date on new releases and news you can sign up for her mailing list here:
http://www.laneeslane.com/?page_id=586

Made in the USA
Monee, IL
05 March 2022